Skin Tight

A Guide To Rubbermen, Macho Fetish and Fantasy

Tim Brough

Skin Tight

A Guide To Rubbermen, Macho Fetish and Fantasy

Second Edition

A Boner Book
Published by The Nazca Plains Corporation
Las Vegas, Nevada
2008

ISBN: 978-1-887895-62-0

Published by

The Nazca Plains Corporation ®
4640 Paradise Rd, Suite 141
Las Vegas NV 89109-8000

Art Direction, Blake Stephens

Acknowledgements

There is nothing a journalist dreads more than to have to write about the loss or passing of a close friend, family member or co-worker. Yet in the Spring of 1999, I had to confront all three. Peter "Rubber Bear" Tolos was the first man to induct me into the rubber scene, and it was his idea to get me working on *Rubber Rebel* in 1994. When he suffered his fatal heart attack in February 1999, I was not sure if I wanted to keep *Vulcan America* on track.

I'd had two other occasions where I'd been tested with this kind of assignment. The first was during my radio days when a close friend in the recording industry died in a plane crash. I wrote a short piece for him in the magazine I was working for at the time. The second was when the man who brought me into the leather scene, Paul "Papa Bear" Sehm succumbed to cancer in 1994. My farewell to him appeared in *The Leather Journal*. But at the time of Peter's passing, I had to buck up and promise the readers of *Vulcan America* that I would continue. I had a horrible time reconciling that the Bear was no longer in my life and our project would succeed without him in the house. It wasn't always easy, but the title continued for 18 issues.

One of the reasons I finished *Skin Tight: A Guide to Rubbermen Macho Fetish and Fantasy* was to honor Peter's memory. He did so many things that easily pass into history and end up forgotten. And despite the fact that *Vulcan America* was kind of a one-man show, you can never have too many friends and enough help. Thanks to so many of you over the years who have helped me spread awareness of rubber, and that includes just about anyone whose name appears anywhere in this book, but not exclusively limited to those persons.

Additonal thanks to Ryan Johnson and Rubber Willi for extra help with the history and contest chapters, and Frank Blondale for photo permission.

To some of my best friends in the world. Papa Snake, Uncle Ed, Jack Rinella and family, Butch, Bert The Bear, Sir Larry and slave barb, Jazz and Stewart, Dr. Bob and family, Bob Genz, Jim Madden; The Bike Stop, Outwrite Bookstore Atlanta, Andrew, Larry, Paul Swycord and Daddy Doug in Atlanta, Master Gerry, Master Thomas, Alex Ironrod, Master Conrad and slave kat, Master Malik and Catherine, Musician Mark Weigle, Filmmaker Paul Bright, Artist Joe Patton, StationHouse Leathers, Dragon's Lair Productions, CLAW,

Phil "When it's tight it's right!" Ross and anyone who got me through life in general.

　　　　And always, love to my family and to my Papa Joel.

In Memoriam: Jonathan Patrick Hayden
August 3, 1968 - November 16, 2006

Dedication

To Roger Hickey and David Boyer.

In 1996, you started a tradition at The Cell Block Chicago with the first Rubber Blowout Weekend. And it has continued. Thanks to you, Gentlemen, Rubber found a fertile place in America to grow and thrive.

Skin Tight: Rubbermen, Macho Fetish and Fantasy is humbly decidated to you, the work that you and all members of the Cell Block staff put into those early weekends, and to your generosity to me over these many years.

Skin Tight

A Guide To Rubbermen, Macho Fetish and Fantasy

Contents

Flexible Tautness:
Why Rubbermen Love Their Fetish

It can be hard as armor plate. It can be spongy and soft like cloth padding. It can wrap around your body and hug as close as a reptilian second layer of skin. A good craftsman can fashion the finest of clothing from the widest variation of the same materials. It can be cheap, it can cost you plenty. It can make you feel hypermasculine, or it can make someone you wouldn't cast a second glance in everyday situations attractive as a superhero.

You probably thought I was talking about leather. I wasn't. I was referring to rubber.

Rubber holds an intense attraction for men whose fetish developed around it. As the editor of America's largest male rubberist magazine, I frequently would get letters from men attempting to put their love for rubber into words. Some told me stories of using their mother's dishwashing gloves to wrap around their dicks as youngsters. I've been sent stories about how men would sneak off to the barn or garage where they would masturbate while pressed against innertubes or tires. For many of us, it wasn't a learned behavior. There was just something about the old gasmask in the attic or that tire swing, or the first pair of shiny black buckling galoshes that triggered an unexplainable segment of the brain, the one that sends cascades of hormones to the appropriate reactive body zone. But why? How does something as simple as a photo of men in diving suits trigger such an intensively private erotic response for so many people?

Rubber is like leather in many aspects where talk of the fetish reflex is concerned. Like most difficult-to-explain responses, you have to break it down to the five senses, which is what I'll try to do here. First and most obvious is smell. There is nothing that can trigger the auto response of a hardcore rubberman like the scent of a closet or cabinet filled with well-cleaned rubber. Good, high quality rubber will have its own sexual musk to it, and it's that reminder of what you're about to give yourself that can get a rubberman aroused. In the way a Thanksgiving dinner in the oven can set one to salivating, for many, rubber smells of sex. Couple that with many rubber fetishists' love of blue-collar gear (hazardous material [hazmat] suits, electronic protection gear, firemen, aviators and the like) or athletic gear (sport team suits, pads and plates, surf or dive wear), and there is the scent of men engaging in hyper-male activity. To find a vintage firejacket that still has the smell of smoke from the job embedded in the rubber will set many a man's eyes rolling. It's the smell of men doing what a "real man" does, and for many, a strong image to turn on to.

Sight: What could be more exciting than a man who has spent count-less hours working his body into human sculpture flaunting himself for you? Dressing him in a manner that accentuates that effort. Rubber clothes do that for anyone! Even the most lenient of the physically fit can suddenly become a smooth, shining body of male muscle culture. Men who dream of being a superman can do that by buying a tight-fitting, hot shining gleaming rubber tank top, fitting so close to the body that every move he makes follows the contours of the body. Gym bunny or no, a good piece of rubber brings out the look of your masculinity. A few hot pieces of gear will turn you into a man you imagine yourself to be, as well. You are no longer a mild-mannered accoun-tant somewhere...you have become a fireman or a fighter pilot. To a greater extreme, many rubber/latex fetishists will collect enough gear to become a superhero. Rubber and latex comes in so many colors that it lends itself to those kinds of visuals. I know of several men who have comic book hero fantasies and have worked meticulously to create a perfect Batman outfit or a fully coordinated Mighty Morphin Power Ranger suit. Or even a professional football player. Rubber is much more flexible than leather when it comes to hypermale image projection, when every night on the town becomes an exten-sion of a personality.

So you've put on the tightest rubber pants and T-shirt you own, you've covered it with a gritty pair of coveralls you bought secondhand after knowing that it was used on the streets of the city by some hot-looking and male-smelling, gritty, tough cigar-smoking DWP (Department of Water and Power) forklift operator. You're at the top of your game and you're going to find someone who will respond to your ideal. But how does it feel?

Those tight rubber pants never stop touching you, and neither will your shirt. Rubber can cocoon you in a manner that no other material can even approximate. Sexually, it becomes not what you take off, but how much you have on. Just a tiny bit of lube will provide you massage for the entire evening and you don't even have to touch yourself. Your body supplies the vibrations. For a rubber fetishist, rubber can give you the kind of feel desired to trigger the reaction you know you want. Be it the sweaty massage that long-term latex wearing will bring to the heavy, encompassing wrap that seven or eight layers of suiting will deliver to a scene, gear can present it all to you. Heat, danger, enlightenment, deprivation, submission, domination...rubber in any combination permits its fanatics to have it all. You feel like your own man when you put on your favorite gear and suit up for the day's activities...or get someone else suited up and ready for an evening's worth of gaming.

There's another aspect to the feel of rubber. To a touch-sensitive body, a tight rubber garment will "spread" the touch against it. Because of the flexibility of rubber, once it clings to your body, a rub against it will reverberate along your flesh underneath. Should you and a partner be pressing on or feeling each other, imagine how the fingers stroking against your back would feel if the spreading waves from the rubber were moving all along your spine and not just stopping at your partner's fingertips. Should your scene move into kinkier realms of bondage or sensory deprivation, a rubber hood over the head sends trippy sweeping sensations around the head as it is stroked, a blindfold removes all but the pressures of those touches while transmitting the waves of pleasure/torments that you're striving for. Because of rubber's flexible tautness, a man drawn up inside a sleepsack or mummified in those deliciously scented rubber straps can push and stretch for all he's worth, but as the rubber slacklessly returns to its given shape and the bottom remains trapped inside, his bindings contoured to his body and as unforgiving as a second skin, rubber again provides a sensual trigger that is unlike any other source material. With rubber outfits of different styles, the amount of pressure or severity of a blow varies as well. Imagine a bondage scene where the chest or shoulders of your intended target are protected enough that the pounding of chains against his body will do no more than bounce away with a loud thud and a man inside submitting to your blows!

We come to the last two of our rubber fetishist sensoral guidelines then, sound and taste. Sound is the easier to explain in some manner, because of the way we are used to defining sounds we enjoy (or at least recognize). When rubber is struck, it has a wonderfully unique snapping sound, or a certain kind of smack that cloth of any variety can't replicate. A rubber-covered body becomes a bizarre form of human percussion instrument because of this feature. The sound of a hand being pulled along a tightly-stretched, slick, rubberized body will drive any rubberman into a Pavlovian state of drooling; again, being inside that rubber as it is being "sounded" can drive you to fits. Not just because of the sound itself, but from the combinations. The noise as it conveys the coming excitement, the feel as it moves along the body (should you be wearing a hood, this pairing is rubber ecstasy), and the smell as heat and excitement builds rubber and sweat to inflammatory levels. The kind of rubber used can also make a difference in the sound: thick neoprene, because of its spongy nature, has a sound all its own.

Taste is probably a harder one to define. I have a friend whose rubber boot fetish is so deeply ingrained that he can tell you which brand of boots are in his mouth...just by chewing on the rims. There are many men who do not consider a scene complete unless a rubber-gloved thumb is shoved in his mouth. Or better yet, a thick latex dildo or rubber ball gag. For these rubberists, it's just as much the completeness of the rubber coverage. All the cavities of the body are touched by rubber, inside and out, that bring these extremes into the forefront of their rubber desires. Their ass is plugged with rubber, a lubed sheath covers their cock and balls, rubber has entered their mouths, their hands are gloved with heavy industrial gloves, boots ride high on their legs, a gas mask covers the face. For a rubber fetishist, it hardly becomes a question of why. It becomes the answer to how...how to bring back that feeling of power, how to gain control of my image for just this moment, how to derive the greatest sensation of pleasure. Yet most rubberists, like just about any fetishist, would be hard-pressed to give you a ready analysis of what rubber really does for them. So your best bet if you've had a rubber interest or if you just have the curiosity is not to try to define it, but to just enjoy what it brings to you and where the resulting exploration will take you.

Rubbercare: Two Views

View One:
A LIFE IN RUBBER: WEAR AND CARE
By Paul "Aqualaboy"

WHY RUBBER?

"Smell the Glove!"

Latex - neoprene - rubber - gummi. Casual - formal - industrial. By any name, in any style, a man in rubber is hot. Sight, smell, touch, even the taste and sound of it: rubber stimulates all the senses. One gaze on a man in rubber, my heart races and I am quicksand. Lean hard muscle under a smooth slick rubber skin; well-fitting rubber sculpts a man into a living, breathing, liquid statue. Whether on the dance floor or in the back rooms, at home or at the Opera, the man in rubber commands attention. Rubber forms a smooth sculpted contour of the human male. Glistening jet-black rubber gives a man an edgy alien look that few fetish materials can match.

Rubber can release intense hidden passions, both sensual and sexual. The smell of rubber is intoxicating, not the industrial smell of a tire store, but the sweet smell of pure natural rubber. Mix in some mansweat and cum and let it stew for a couple of hours and you've got a heady brew. For the man wearing it, rubber is sensually unrelenting. Rubber clings to and slides over his body and all its parts, scintillating the skin in its encapsulating embrace. Whether tight or loose fitting, rubber amplifies sensations. If you have not experienced a full massage in rubber, it is your charge to do so as soon as possible.

For some, rubber gear takes a man back to his boyhood fantasies. I still recall getting hard as a fencepost as we drove past construction workers in their yellow rubber boots in the snowy streets of Buffalo. My biggest fantasies, though, were about being trapped underwater in those antique copper helmets and rubber deep-sea diving suits, struggling to escape some underwater trap while fighting a massive hard-on.

Whether you've never tried rubber wear or gear before, just purchased your first rubber piece, or have been a hard-core rubberman for years, you should find something new in this chapter. True, the sensations offered by rubber are not to everyone's taste, but if you have not tried it, perhaps it is time to reconsider. Rubber might surprise you. Some of our best rubber friends were rubber skeptics. The information and advice described here will hopefully dispel a few myths. This chapter is based on more than two decades of personal experience, and may help you make choices in your new fetish or find new pleasures that you may have been missing.

The Rubber Lifestyle

It has been said rubber is an investment. Rubber is not cheap: quality costs, and quality rubber requires some skill to make. A basic t-shirt will set you back $60-150, depending on accents, but the feel of hot damp rubber on the skin, and the extra attentions from friends and strangers more than offset the costs. The financial investments are easy to calculate and to control, theoretically. It may be expensive, but it is much better for you physically and emotionally, cheaper in the long run, and sure beats the fuck out of a drug habit!

The rubber lifestyle can also require an emotional investment, but this investment is (or in some cases not!) controlled by you. Rubber can be a sometime thing, brought out for special occasions or for rubber play in the privacy of your own home. But, if you are a rubber pig like myself, little else matters. Rubber for sleep, rubber to mow the lawn or paint the house, rubber at the supermarket, rubber is all encompassing for a true rubber pig. For such men, the care and maintenance of their rubber is an integral part of that lifestyle.

Your High Maintenance Friend?

Rubber wear and rubber care are intimately linked, and can be a powerful mechanism to intimacy. Rubber as fetish wear is generally regarded as higher maintenance than most, if not all, fetish wear, such as leather, PVC, underwear, socks, or hazmat. Rubber is a natural organic substance with limited durability and chemical stability. Exposure to the environment initiates a slow decay process that can be arrested but never halted. Following some of the suggestions outlined in this chapter, you can keep your rubber strong and supple for 10 years or more. Under the right conditions, rubber can last several decades.

Rubber can require maintenance, yet there are plenty of myths associated with this aspect. *Rubber takes several hours to put on. I will have to do all sorts of tedious maintenance on my rubber. Rubber disintegrates in the sun.* As an open-minded anti-fascist/Taliban/Puritan type, I will tell you there are no absolute answers to these or any other questions, so let's explore.

RUBBER WEAR AND CARE

Buying Your Rubber

Where to start? Rubber's versatility is unmatched. From rubber jeans and shirts to jockstraps, harnesses, fireman's raincoats (before gore-tex at least), diving suits, and hip boots, to rubber gloves, gags, butt-plugs, and the ever-popular gasmask, there is almost no garment or gear that is not available in rubber. And that's just a small sample. Rubber's strength, flexibility, elasticity, and watertight properties make it perfect for wear and play. It is also inflatable! An inflated rubber hood or body bag (or any rubber gear for that matter) can radically add to the sense of restraint. And there is the vast array of rubber sex toys in all sizes shapes and colors. When it comes to interpersonal relations, rubber's elastic properties and resistance to fluids give it a flexibility and range few materials can match. When is the last time you let someone piss all over your leathers?

Rubber comes in almost every form and style for almost any fetish. Industrial or uniform rubber is intensely masculine. Tight-fitting smooth black rubber is like walking around naked, a long black rubber trench coat like walking off the set of *The Matrix*. Many styles can be found, and all you need is a search engine and your imagination. Full dress rubber, as radical as a full tuxedo, is also available for an evening at the Opera. Rubber toy and garment vendors are proliferating in the new Internet age. I will not make specific recommendations here; my partner and I have had both good and bad experiences. I do have some recommendations that will help make rubber purchasing easier. A good place to start is some of the on-line rubber groups and clubs, starting with RubberZone, many of which have detailed listings and links.

Some vendors sell molded rubber garments. These are made as one piece by an injection process. While usually cheaper, they are subject to variations in thickness and quality and may not fit as well or look as sharp as a tailored garment. Unless dealing with second-hand items, the old rule "You get what you pay for" applies.

Tailored garments are made from separate pieces glued together at seams. It is also easier to design colored or patterned rubberwear this way. Some rubber is stitched together but is guaranteed to tear at the seams unless reinforced on the backside. Verify that seams are backed if a garment is stitched. Personally, I prefer tailored rubber, but molded rubber can be a fair choice if you are concerned about cost or are unsure if the rubber fetish is where you want to go.

Gasmasks and other fetish gear are in abundance in military surplus stores, one of the rubber fetishist's top destinations. Surplus stores are hit-and-miss, however. Some carry major items like survival suits, gloves, and rubber Mickey Mouse boots (I prefer the ones without valves); other stores just have khakis, fatigues and combat boots. A trip to your sporting goods shop or hardware store may lead you to some basic rubber hip boots and waders. Your local safety equipment vendors will have floor models and catalogs of some excellent industrial boots, gloves and suits. EBay and similar on-line auction houses are now the ultimate source for the more unusual rubber fetish goods, including hip-boots, hazmat, diving suits, fire, rain gear and just about anything else.

Fit, Color, Thickness

For tight rubber, fit is everything. If at all possible, try it on first. For most, sojourning to Berlin, London or San Francisco just to try on a pair of rubber pants is not practical, so you must order online or by phone. On arrival, shower first and keep the piece clean in case it must be returned. Not all makers will accept returns, however. If you prefer a looser fit, all you need is a size. Be aware that large in the UK is not necessarily a large in the US or on the continent. Send the vendor your measurements when you order to be sure. If you routinely take a stock size off the rack at Neiman-Marcus, then you should be okay with standard sizes in rubber; but if you are an odd size, then custom may be the only way to go (pricing policies on custom vary widely). An email in advance is the best assurance on sizing. Rubber is notorious for revealing every physical attribute. This is not necessarily a bad thing. There are plenty of men out there who like other men of all sizes and shapes, be they bears or beanpoles. Beauty is all relative, so don't let the narrow vision of a few limit you. Wear your rubber!

Designer latex comes in many colors, including red, yellow, white, black, brown, blue, khaki, and clear, among others. The lighter colors will stain more easily. Camo and patterned latex material is also becoming available. Yellow, red, and white rubber can even be part of your hanky code. Clear latex is flesh tone and translucent, so most everything is visible. It will discolor over time, however, becoming more yellowish.

Rubber comes in a range of thicknesses, measured in millimeters (typically 1-3 mm for most commercially available garments). Each has its pros/cons. The thinnest grade (0.4 to 0.5 mm) is more easily torn when snagged, requiring extra care while donning. It can also fall victim to the random rubber-snapping idiot on the street. But thin rubber also conforms to and hugs the body more tightly, allowing you to show off that hot ass or bulge. Thicker rubber is more resilient and less likely to dry rot. It provides a more intense feeling of constriction and resistance, a real turn-on especially in the form of a straightjacket or full body suit. Thick rubber gives less and can sometimes leave rashes or blisters on the edge after long-term wear. Jeans are typically 1-2 mm. Heavy diving suits, flight suits, or straightjackets are typically 2-3 mm. The combination of fit and thickness will evolve as your rubber experience increases.

American rubber makers are required by law to use weaker rubber glues than those used in Europe or Japan. As a result, glued seams occasionally begin to separate after a few years, but this has not prevented us from enjoying their products. Some vendors will reglue their seams (or you can attempt this yourself – see below). Countering this is the tendency in recent years for European rubber vendors to charge outrageously for shipping, sometimes more than 25% of the base cost. There is no shipping, of course, if you go there yourself.

Dressing in Rubber

Like all other facets of this fetish, dressing is what you make of it. It does not require hours to get into a rubber outfit, unless you are planning to wear a couple of dozen pieces of gear, or doing a long photo shoot. You can be fully dressed in 10 minutes or less. The secret is to let dressing be part of the fun.

If possible, let someone help you dress. Like the armor-clad knights of old, being dressed for "battle" by your "squire" is a powerful male ritual. I experience this feeling every time I am dressed by my tenders into my 200-pound copper, lead, and rubber deep-sea diving helmet and suit. Whether facing a knight in combat, the dangers of the deep, or a heavy night of sling action, being dressed in rubber by a friend, partner, or lover is intensely masculine. Let it flow through you and charge you emotionally and physically!

If you are on your own, don't let that tight rubber T-shirt intimidate you! Whether you are planning a solo act at home or cruising at the local leather bar, dressing by yourself can be just as stimulating. Here are some tips to make it easier.

Dressing in rubber is just like dressing in street clothes, with a few important exceptions. Lubrication is not required, but it does make dressing in tight rubber much easier. Lubrication prevents sticking and reduces skin irritation during extended wear. This can take the form of a light dusting of unscented talc or powdered J-Lube inside the garment. French chalk can be used if available. Do not use cornstarch, as it has been linked to some latex allergies. If a choking cloud of powder spreads across the room, you've probably used too much!

If you don't like powders, try a wet lube. The shower is one way; you will be wet inside for a while, but more than likely you will be sweaty anyway before the evening is out. Alternatively, lightly coat the inside of the garment or your skin with glycerin or a silicone-based body oil or body glide, again unscented and latex safe! Various brands are available, including, but not limited to, Eros and GunOil, which can be found at most leather, rubber, and sex shops. Several online distributors specialize in lubes. Good quality body glides and oils can also be therapeutic for the skin. Avoid all petroleum-based products. Wipe off excess talc or lube as required. A little goes a long way. Pour a few drops into the palm of your hand and spread it across your torso or the inside of the garment. Here is where a partner or helper can be handy for the back and other areas. Let it be a sensual experience for both parties. As we will see, the same is true for polishing.

Natural sweating can make the inside of your rubber a personal sauna: rubber doesn't breathe. Sweaty rubber is one of the most intense aspects of the fetish for some rubbermen. Some sweat heavily, some hardly at all. After five minutes in the sun, you will probably be soaked inside your rubber, and that's how I like it! A few might regard this as distasteful, but a hot heavy night with your partner would likely leave you sweaty and steamy anyway, so why not enjoy it? Sweat can act as a natural lube, allowing the rubber to slide more freely, which can be highly stimulating and pleasurable in certain areas. And the dank sweaty masculine smell of worn rubber as you take it off is indescribable (the editor rejected scratch-and-sniff cards for this book, so you will have to imagine this part).

Most gear is easy to don, but tight zipperless shirts usually present the greatest challenge. Once powdered or lubed, try rolling or bunching the shirt before inserting head and then each arm; unroll once it is over the head.

Do trim and buff your nails before donning your rubber, and remove all sharp body jewelry. Try not to poke a hole in the rubber with your fingers: grasp firmly but carefully. Nothing elicits an unwelcome curse faster than tearing an expensive rubber garment with nails or studs. Or simply go with a zippered shirt for ease of donning.

The keys to pain-free rubber dressing:
- Lubricate (pure talc or baby powder, liquid water-based lubes, water.
- Remove or trim sharp or pointed jewelry and sharp nails.
- Ask a mate or friend, if possible.
- Roll up a tight shirt, put it on, unroll it.

Polishing Your Rubber

Polishing rubber is always optional. Some prefer the natural unvarnished look and touch of natural rubber. I like any rubber, but usually prefer the brilliant sheen of a smooth glossy polish. A proper polish gives you and your rubber the impression of being living liquid, and you might be confused with the black slime creatures of *Varga II*.

Polish also helps protect rubber from UV exposure and other elements of decay. Stick to silicone-based or other polish formulated for natural latex. Oil-based polishes are a big faux pas and will leave you with a gooey black mass instead of rubber. Avoid rubber polishes marketed for automotives. Some are formulated in such a way as to require continual polishing or the rubber decays rapidly. Some of these polishes may work, but the jury is still out, and it is best to be cautious with fine rubber that can cost several hundred dollars. Spend a few dollars more for the right stuff. Polishes include pure silicone, formulated latex polish (a milky silicone-based solution), and ultra slick high-grade lubes (such as Wet Platinum). Liquid silicone and slick lubes give a high gloss polish that lasts longest.

Good latex polishes can be found at most leather shops (and I don't mean sofas), rubber shops (usually located only in the largest cities), erotic shops, and scuba shops. Liquid silicone, usually sold in large spray cans, can be found in similar locations, or where food preparation supplies or lubricants are sold. Be sure to ask for food-grade silicone only! Call ahead. Shoeshine sponges with silicone are sometimes used. If you are unsure, try it first on a small corner to make sure the liquid does not damage your rubber.

The act of polishing is a sometimes neglected art in rubber life. The rush to get out the door can sometimes mean a quick spray-on or wipe. If you have time, I recommend a slow sensual approach. You can polish before or after the rubber is on, but if you're on your own, you may need to polish the back beforehand anyway. Not everyone has long arms. Spray a few shots of polish on each side, doing one section at a time. Using a clean for-rubber-only dense weave rag, sponge, or shop towel (see auto stores), gently rub the polish into the rubber. Repeat for the pants or bottoms. There isn't much trick to it, just work it to a smooth finish. The rubberman underneath probably won't mind the rubdown. An alternative to sponges or rags is to use your hands. Remove your rings first if possible. You can imagine how sensual for both parties rubbing another man's rubber-clad chest or ass can be. Polishing may thus require additional working to achieve a uniform coat!

Trial and error will show you what works best for you. Don't over-polish or you will look like a bad paint job. Polish or slick lubes can be used separately or in combination. Some of my friends use latex polish as a cleaner, followed by a high gloss coat of silicone or slick lubes.

The keys to effective rubber polishing:
- avoid oil-based products.
- use latex polish, liquid silicone or slick lubes (Wet Platinum, for example).
- use a dense rag, sponge, or hands and just rub it in.
- enjoy!

Wearing Rubber

Two things: remember where you are going, and grease is your enemy. Rubber attracts attention like nothing else, but not everyone is fetish tolerant. Be aware of your surroundings and avoid areas where you might attract unwanted attention. Dress for the occasion and location. Fortunately, in most cities these areas are usually well known and avoidable. But do be prepared for a quick getaway or a cell phone if a gang of drunken teenagers with something to prove crosses your path.

The buffet table or snack machine can expose your rubber to all sorts of nasty grease and food. Splattered food will not cause permanent harm if removed within short order, although it may leave a temporary pucker. Find warm water and a very mild or diluted soap and remove the offending particles with a towel. Wipe again with just water. Spit works very well, too. If you've been heavily pawed over during your adventures, a good hand rinse at home will help prevent those oily fingerprints from becoming permanent. Lighter colors in rubber, such as white or yellow, stain more easily.

Cigarettes represent a serious threat to rubber. Hot ashes will permanently scar rubber. The smoky odor will come out after a long steamy shower, however.

Won't it stick or pull on my body hair? This is a common technical question I am asked (*Aren't you hot in that?* is the runaway winner – or loser – on the most common question list). Being nearly hairless, I have no personal experience in this, but my friends confirm that silicone lube or body glide reduces or eliminates this problem. Shaving may not be an option for you, but lubes will do a good job during both dressing and wear. Some of you may need more lube on your hairy parts than others.

Heat and Sun, Cold and Wind

Yes, it is true. Natural latex does not like direct sun, but it will not crumble or go gooey from limited exposure. My partner and I have worn rubber out in daylight for several hours at a time with no ill effects, although we do avoid standing around in direct sunlight. Long-term or repeated sun exposure is most definitely damaging to rubber and latex, however, and can alter or fade some colors.

Rubber does not breathe! A shorty suit will allow some cooling by sweat evaporation from your arms and legs, but heat will build up fast in a full body suit if you are involved in heavy physical activities or are exposed to direct sun or warm temperatures. Hydrate! If you are restrained in any way and likely to overheat, it is important that your partner have a fan and a spray bottle of water handy to spray you down. Evaporative cooling will help keep you from overheating. Exercise simple caution and prudence: monitor each other for signs of heat stress. Be wary of situations where you may be susceptible to overheating. Have options to get out of the heat or have cool water or air nearby.

I actually like going out in the Sun in rubber. The sweltering southern heat hasn't stopped us from going out in full rubber in summer, but some precaution is advised. Rubber in daylight is like wearing a personal sauna. There are two aspects to consider: sweat and heat. The warm bath of sweat inside your hot rubber can be intensely stimulating and is often part of a rubberman's mantra. I love the feel of a pint of sweat sloshing in each rubber boot, and the feel of a bead of sweat running down my crack is a rush. Rubber, especially black rubber, rapidly absorbs the Sun's heat. The rubber will become hot to the touch in a matter of seconds. The intense heat pouring into your body from all sides is an amazing sensation, one to which I am becoming addicted to. Direct sun can't be sustained for very long, however, due to the intense skin heat, so be sure a shady haven is available nearby.

The opposite of heat is cold. Sheet latex has no insulating properties whatsoever, and can feel like going out naked in a snowstorm. In fact, it can feel like sheets of ice against your skin. The wind especially will strip you of any insulating warm air surrounding you. We have wandered the streets of Toronto and Chicago in winter in our rubber. The notorious cold winds of winter can feel like ten thousand needles poking the skin at once, intense but quite exhilarating in its own perverse way.

Multiple layering helps mitigate the chill a little bit, but you might consider a leather or cold-weather jacket. Drysuits and foam neoprene wet-suits are okay in the cold if you like them. Hypothermia is the main risk, so avoid prolonged marches in the cold. Take a subway or taxi if more than a few blocks.

It bears repeating: avoid extended solar exposure, but carry water, and hydrate.

Rubber and Your Skin

I have been in rubber continuously for as long as 7 days and am currently on a 5-day rubber bender as I sit here editing. While highly stimulating and erotic, such long exposure to moisture is not normally good for the skin. I am most sensitive to rubber where I sit. Irritation is usually due to repetitive sliding of the rubber against the skin. The best solution is a good lubricating pre-coat of silicone lubricant such as Eros or other body oils (latex safe, of course) on your sensitive areas. If you have sensitive skin, or develop a rash whenever you sweat, rubber may not be for you, or at least not for long exposure. If you like long-term encapsulation, take an occasional shower to rinse away the grime between you and the rubber. Otherwise, the skin is resilient and, with proper care, your outer layers will enjoy many years of rubber fun.

Latex allergies are uncommon, but they exist and can be severe. The origins are unclear, and I am not a medical doctor. The most frequently cited cause is the use of cornstarch as a dry lubricant in rubber gloves. Avoid cornstarch at all costs, and avoid any medical gloves that are not labeled as allergy free. Don't wear rubber over open sores or cuts.

Where the Rubber Meets the Road: Going Public

Rubber in public has been our signature. My mate and I live in a large southern city, and we wear it everywhere. The response to public rubber varies from silent stares to outright amazement. So many have come up to greet us, take a pic, or chat, that I've lost count. Oddly, the only difficulty we have ever encountered occurred one night in London, rubber capital of Europe, involving some drunk teenagers looking for trouble. Our best advice is to dress for the occasion and location. Most people enjoy seeing something new under the sun, but remember your audience. Don't go looking for trouble, and chances are it won't find you.

Wearing rubber overseas is not only possible, but almost a requirement! With few exceptions, Europe has not seen the rise of Puritanism that the US has. I have worn my rubber many times in the streets and on the trains. I have even worn my black rubber on AMTRAK here in the States. In fact, I am in the lounge car on a train in Arizona, wearing a rubber sleeveless-T, pouch shorts and chaps as I write this section. Public rubber in most of Africa and in Islamic or non-western Catholic countries is strongly discouraged, however.

There are several things to consider when traveling with rubber. The beginning of the 21st century has seen a violent resurgence of religious extremism and the smothering of tolerance and reason. The policies in Washington are likely to provoke continuing external threats, requiring continued tight air travel security. It is not recommended that you carry on rubber gas masks, hoses or other hard-core fetish items. Security agents have seen everything, but generally are not on the lookout for rubber fetishists (at least not for professional reasons). We have not heard of anyone being hassled for their gear, but fluids and gas-related items are likely to be confiscated from carry-on luggage. Why tempt fate? Pack your gear in your checked luggage. Weight will compress rubber, so rubber should be removed and hung or stowed at the earliest opportunity upon landing.

At this point, I should relate the following experience. My rubber mate returned home following a recent rubber event while I remained overnight. At the airport, realizing he had left his ID with me, he went through security anyway, dressed head to toe in full rubber gear. The agents waved him through, commenting, "He's not hiding anything under that!"

Washing Your Rubber

Your rubber night is over and you've made a (hopefully pleasant) mess of yourself. Time to clean up. Fingerprints, food and other soils can permanently scar rubber. Cum will dry into a hard coating that is difficult to remove from rubber without a good long soak. What to do?

The best place to clean your rubber is in the shower. Let the warm water run over and inside your rubber. Rubbing your suit with a rag or your hands will dislodge most particulate contaminants. A very mild diluted soap can be used if needed but is not usually necessary. Several European rubber dealers sell blue disinfectant soaps designed for latex. Check them out. If you've been in the hot tub, a good long soak in a warm shower will help remove the chlorine. The same is true for residual barroom smoke (especially if you live outside California or New York). If your rubber is still not quite clean, soak it in a plastic tub for several hours using a rubber safe soap if available, then rinse again. If you are not too exhausted, let the clean up be fun! If you've brought a present or future rubberman home with you, I'm quite sure he would be happy to assist you in the shower! Rubbing each other's gear by hand can lead to interesting reactions.

An alternative to the shower is the washing machine. This requires a front-loader, as a top loader will tend to shred rubber. Use lukewarm or cold water and rubber soap (if available). Very diluted Woolite has been suggested as soap, although I have not tried it myself. Of course, your rubber should stay far away from the dryer!

Removing a tight rubber shirt is also best done in the shower. Start with the bottom and pull up. Wet rubber will easily slide off. Rubber tends to cling to itself and trying to roll off a tight shirt dry can turn you into an escape contortionist. The struggle could result in a torn shirt. There is no easy solution to this problem except patience, the showers, or external intervention. Try rolling it up your torso and then pulling one arm out at a time. The rest should follow. However it is done, earrings and jewelry should first be removed.

Keys to pain-free rubber undressing:
- Remove or trim sharp or pointed jewelry and sharp nails
- Ask a mate or friend, if possible
- Roll up a tight shirt, pull it off through the arms first.

"No More Wire Hangers!"

Store rubber dry! That slimy moldy mass you might find inside your gloves or pockets is not only unpleasant but can eat your rubber. Gloves and boots should be inverted for drying. I have punched small holes in the inside bottoms of suit pockets to drain water (this should be done with great care to avoid punching a hole in the front surface). Metal snaps or parts should be dried immediately. Water can chemically react with some metal parts to discolor lighter shades of rubber or cause the rubber itself to become gooey over time.

For storage, there are different philosophies. Joan Crawford would definitely screech if she saw you hanging your fine latex on wire hangers, and justifiably so. The narrow wire can crease the rubber, or react and discolor it. Stick to plastic hangers, the thicker the better. Buff down any of those annoying sharp injection-molding edges or spurs left from manufacture. For pants, pant hangers of wood and metal can also crease the rubber. Try gluing strips of old neoprene wetsuit material or similar foam rubber on the inside of standard wooden pant hangers.

Smaller items like t-shirts, shorts, and gloves can be stored powdered with talc in sealed plastic bags. All rubber should be in as dark, cool, and dry an environment as can be mustered. Hang boots, gloves, and sheaths upside down to speed draining and drying. If the boots are lined, drying will require several days, but must be completed, or mold will form and your feet will not forgive you for a long time.

Rubber Repair

Rubber's one weakness is repair. Once torn, it cannot be restored to its original elasticity and strength at that point. It can be patched and may be watertight again, but the original tear will always be a weak spot, and a patch disrupts the original smooth contours of rubber gear. Nonetheless, at some point you will tear a rubber piece and if not extremely so, a repair is in order and can be achieved effectively.

Some rubber vendors also do repair work (check merchants directly for policies), but you can also try it yourself. Rubber repair is treated much the same as for a bicycle inner tube. Cut a patch of similar gauge rubber about half an inch wider than your tear or hole. (Remember that the patch will show as a raised bump on the external surface, so cut the shape accordingly.) Buff the patch and the garment, usually on the inside and out of sight, with sandpaper in order to help the glue bond stronger. Apply two coats of good rubber glue to both surfaces with a small cheap paintbrush. Let each coat dry 5-10 minutes. With great care, position the patch over the spot. This can be frustrating if the patch hits the glue in the wrong spot. You may need four hands to position a large patch properly.

One important note: if the rubber surface has been polished with silicone-based polishes or lubes, the glue will likely fail to bond properly. Clean the area of the tear thoroughly with rubbing alcohol first. Check online European rubber vendors (starting with Blackstyle) for glues, which are stronger than most available in the states.

Once rubber has gone bad, it can't be saved. Dry rot occurs when the organic polymers break down and the rubber hardens and cracks. Similarly, rubber can go gooey and sticky. This can be due to age, UV exposure, surface contamination, or perhaps it was just a bad batch of latex. The only solution is to cut off the decayed parts plus an extra inch or so, and patch a new section of rubber over the hole.

RUBBER FUN

Liquid Latex

Liquid latex has been available to the pervy public for a few decades now. It can be incredibly hot to be painted in the stuff, forming an intimate bond with the body that even the best-tailored garments can't quite match. Part of the fun is also peeling the layers off later. It can also be used to form molds of certain body parts, including, but not limited to, the hands and feet.

Follow the instructions when applying, but here are a few tips. It is normally applied by a brush, such as the foam brushes found at paint stores. Drying is speeded by use of a hair dryer, although don't overheat the rubber to very high temperatures, as your rubber model will feel everything the rubber does. Add several more coats to achieve the desired thickness, drying as you go. Applying with a painter's airbrush will cool the rubber and add surface tension and tightness. The ammonia used to cure the latex can fill a room: ventilation is recommended.

Several other facts should be kept in mind. While drying and after, the latex victim must not allow one rubber surface to contact another until the latex can be polished. The latex will stick to itself with irreversible results. The other fact concerns hair. Liquid latex will matt hair into a solid mass. You will have to shave that hair off, so it's best to shave your cock and balls first *before* latexing them. A cockring or other devices should maintain hardness. Body hair should also be shaved. Once finished, liquid latex will simply peel off, an interesting sensation in itself. If hair has matted with the latex, a long hot shower and razor blade may help in slowly separating you from the rubber.

Rubber Bondage

The watertight and elastic properties of rubber can enhance any scene involving restraint. Rubber stretches but always fights back to its original shape. It also traps any moisture with you, leaving you helpless to squirm and stew in a pool of your own juices. Rubber restraints come in a variety of forms. For the purist, wrist and ankle restraints come in thick neoprene rubber, although rubber tape can also be used. Be aware not to wrap rubber tape tightly, because the cumulative effect of layered rubber tape can be quite constricting and potentially painful. My favorite rubber restraint is the rubber straightjacket, coupled with hip boots and ankle restraints, squirming in the pools of sweat that drain into the rubber sleeves and boots.

The Vac-Rac is the ultimate in rubber restraint. This device consists of a double layer of rubber into which the bottom slides, and is sealed with a zipper. Air is drawn out with a vacuum pump and the rubber is sucked down tight against the body. Think freezer shrink-wrap; think Han Solo. A Vac-Rac bottom is essentially immobilized and subject to the top's whims. Roving hands slide over the helpless rubberized victim. An air tube is usually passed through a hole into the mouth for breathing.

There are different designs and materials to find on the internet. Some models now have valves that allow you to turn the vacuum off and silence the noise. Most require continuous pumping, which may overheat and shut down an ordinary vacuum. Options include a water vacuum, and portable heat-tolerant vacuums such as the Shark (ultra-silent) and the Runabout. The vacuum will suck the rubber tight to the face. To reduce the pressure, you can experiment with various facemasks or gasmasks, but some will not easily admit a breathing tube, and most will apply pressure on the bridge of the nose. A latex or nylon hood can also reduce ear pressure and noise, although earplugs are not recommended. There is at least one model that allows the head to be free of the rubber (giving the operator greater freedom to experiment with gasmasks, etc.), and a few offer vertical suspension. Our friends in Austin (SlickCo) have come up with several new designs working in three dimensions that suspend the victim in rubber in mid-air!

Diving Gear

Sport, military or commercial diving gear is a major fetish in itself. Diving rubbermen like myself are sometimes called gearheads. Diving is not for the claustrophic or aquaphobic. It also requires a healthy respect for the equipment and the water, and the potentially perilous results of carelessness. A large part of the allure of diving comes from sealing yourself inside a large protective rubber suit and carrying 50 to 200 pounds of life-sustaining gear on your back. That critical dependence on your gear underwater can be very arousing. Many diving rubbermen have done it under the waves. The sense of floating underwater can open new spiritual and physical vistas, producing a profound sense of solitude and isolation underwater, at least until enemy frogmen discover your whereabouts.

Dive gear comes in a variety of colors and configurations. Wetsuits always come in foam neoprene. Many of us more mature rubbermen grew up in the age of smooth-skin black or red wetsuits (think *Thunderball*), and the simple tank/backpack configuration free of today's bulky inflatable buoyancy devices. Most are now made with dull nylon protective linings, but EBay or other resale outlets will get you an old-school unlined suit. Funky sleek wetsuit patterns are increasing in popularity, as the diving world catches up with the fetish world in design. Dry suits, which seal at wrist and neck, are meant to stay dry inside and come in plastic, crushed neoprene, or vulcanized rubber. As a rubberman, I naturally insist on the latter. Dry suits are usually not as sleek as wetsuits but are big turn-ons for gearheads, with air-hoses and valves that intimately integrate the suit, air system and diver into one autonomous unit.

The same feeling of rubber squeezed tight on the skin from a Vac-Rac can be achieved using rubber hip boots in shallow water, or in rubber dry suits. The most famous of these is the Aquala suit (hence my nom-de-plume). This suit is all rubber, in contrast to lined commercial diving suits. Submerging under water will squeeze the air out of the suit. Think of this as a mobile Vac-Rac. I especially enjoy the feeling on leaving the water, the suit tightly squeezed onto my frame. Everything is visible, especially as I do not wear anything underneath. I have spent hours on tropical beaches between dives in my vacuum-sealed Aquala.

Deep-sea diving gear, with helmet, suit, and air hose is also hot. Total enclosure in the massively heavy gear secured inside with heavy leather straps is another way to go. Diving gear is also inflatable. This can be great fun on the surface, as it tends to immobilize your arms, but this should not be attempted underwater without proper planning and scuba training or serious injury will result. Proper scuba instruction is mandatory. Blowing up spread-eagled inside a fully inflated deep-sea diving suit is also great fun but again, training is required.

Use diving gear underwater only with proper scuba training!

Rubber Sex

As much as I love the sensuality of wearing rubber, rubber sex is what I live for. Hot sweaty musky man-sex in full rubber coverage; for many rubbermen, the restricting and encapsulating rubber intensifies their physical response and releases inner passions. Full rubber coverage, capped off with the versatile rubber gas mask, is also excellent for sensory deprivation.

Rubber is well known as a preferred gear for water sports. You can wallow in piss all night and the rubber keeps coming back for more. Rinse it afterwards, and the rubber will last for many a session. In fact, you can wallow in any bodily fluids in rubber. If the rubber suit is sealed at all ends, you need not come into contact with the offending fluids at all, or you can trap it inside the suit with you for the duration, depending on who is pissing on whom. Rubber is also popular for mud-play. A fine debris-free mud is usually best if you wish to keep your gear in good shape. Slime pits are gaining in popularity. Essentially just plastic or rubber sheets (or a shallow pool) smeared with lubricant, such pits allow two or more guys to wrestle in their gear to the mutual enjoyment of all! Think of it as Rubber Twister. A mixed bottle of J-lube goes a long way. The air and watertight properties of rubber open major possibilities no other material offers.

Sling play and bondage in rubber? Major hot! Struggling against his restraints, a rubber bottom (that is to say, me!) will squirm in its all-encompassing embrace, sweating profusely, and loving it. Put on a gasmask and he enters another world. Have a spray bottle of water handy to keep him from overheating. Monitor his condition! Ropes and paddles are all perfectly fine on rubber, but be wary. When removing ropes, please avoid the act of rapidly pulling the ropes over the rubber, which can cause permanent rope burns on the rubber. Leather restraints, paddles, or whips can be used but will scar rubber if applied too vigorously, but you are not likely wearing your Opera rubber in the dungeon anyway, so don't worry too much about it. Just about any leather play toy can be found in rubber, including whips and paddles. Similarly, studded metal instruments can be highly stimulating, but can puncture or tear rubber. All these toys can be used on rubber, but should be used with greater care. Rubber is more fragile than leather, but most likely your play rubber will not be used for public wear anyway!

I enjoy short intense sets on the weight training machine in my short rubbers. The tight rubber rippling across my skin triggers an adrenaline rush and motivates my workout, but caution is required! Longer sets and extended aerobics will raise body temperature and result in dehydration. Do not use full-length rubber, hydrate, and limit your time. Monitor yourself, and start modestly with short exercise periods before working up to longer sets.

My number one recommendation is for you to get a massage or rub-down while wearing a full rubber suit.

The Short List

Yes, it is true that rubber requires more care than a pair of leather chaps or most other fetish materials. Despite this, the feeling and sensation of rubber make rubber care worth all the effort. There are certainly rubbermen who do not regularly polish or clean their rubber, making this part of their rubber identity. For many rubbermen, rubber care is an integral part of their identity as rubbermen. Rubbermen command attention most everywhere they go. Rubbermen are a proud race. Their rubber should reflect their pride. I have offered many useful tips above for maintaining your rubber at its finest and protecting your investment. Here is a short list of the 10 most important things to remember:

1. Try rubber for fit before buying, if possible; be truthful and complete when giving measurements.
2. Lightly lubricate before donning tight-fitting rubber (unscented talc or latex-safe lube).
3. Remove sharp objects and trim nails before dressing and undressing; roll up shirts before inserting arms
4. Unroll tight shirts and pull arms through one at a time; a shower helps during removal.
5. Ask a friend to help!
6. Use non-petroleum-based lubes and polishes (avoid auto store polishes).
7. Short duration solar exposure is okay; avoid prolonged direct Sun exposure.
8. Clean with lukewarm water; a mildly diluted soap can be used if thoroughly rinsed.
9. Lightly polish and/or talc; store on plastic hanger or in bags in cool, dark, dry place; No wire hangers!
10. Be proud of being a rubberman; respect others and have fun!

Because of its waterproof properties, rubber opens almost limitless possibilities for kink and fun. Now that you have the proper information in hand, the next time you dress and are not rushed for time, do it slowly and remember the sensual aspects of rubber. You may end up staying at home that night!

A Boner Book

View Two:
LATEX WEAR AND CARE
FROM THE WEST COAST
By Alan Stroik

There are as many suggestions on how to put on, take off, shine and store your latex as there are rubbermen and women willing to give that advice. I did a lot of research, visited many web sites, talked to rubberpervs and rubber makers to try and find a consensus on how to wear, care and store your rubber. The only consensus I was able to find was on storing your rubber. Everyone else had numerous ideas, thoughts and suggestions on how to wear and care for your rubber clothing.

I will attempt to give as many of the most common techniques as possible. Read all the information, try everything and decide for yourself what works best for you. Wearing rubber is about enjoying the feel of the rubber as it touches your skin, the sensual and erotic nature of it. The tingle when someone rubs your rubber clad body. It is also about getting down and dirty with your fellow rubber pigs. So read, learn and have fun.

Putting On Your Rubber

There are four main schools of thought on donning your rubber: lube, talc, bare or wet. The other decision for men is to shave or not to shave. A lot of rubbermen prefer a smooth, shaved body; it makes the rubber easier to slide on. Many rubbermen shave their entire body before putting on their rubber. I do not shave my body, I tend to get very bad ingrown hairs and have yet to find a solution to avoid that.

Lube: The best lubes are silcone-based or J-Lube. Do **not** use water-based lube; it will dry out and leave you feeling as if the rubber is permanently stuck to your body. You want the rubber to be able to slide on your body for maximum erotic feel. Coat your body with a nice layer of your favorite lube. There are many great silicone based lubes available. Ask your local leather or adult toy store what lube they have. You can even ask them if they have one that works best for putting on rubber.

Talc or corn flour: My preference here is unscented talc. I personally have never tried corn flour but there are many who say it is very effective. Using a makeup puff (a larger sized one), liberally coat your body in the powder.

Bare: No real prep is needed here. You just put your rubber on and you are ready to go.

Wet: A lot of my fellow rubber pigs will jump in the shower and put gear on while standing under a steady stream of water. The water creates a slick barrier between you and the rubber, allowing it to slide on easily. The only down side is that you have to get that water out after the rubber is on. This might cause you to leave a dripping trail of water as you wander around the house as you finish getting ready to head out on the town.

Once you are ready to put your rubber on, you want to be very careful not to stretch or bunch up the rubber too much. Rubber can be very delicate and will rip and tear at the most unfortunate of times. Rubber is naturally stretchy, but if you stretch it too much you will need to go shopping for a replacement piece.

Slowly pull it up or down your body (depending on what you are putting on). If you are having a lot of trouble putting a garment on, you may need more powder or lube. If it bunches anywhere, very gently attempt to unroll the rubber. *NEVER PULL HARD!* If the legs or arms are not stretching up all the way to your crotch or shoulder, start to slowly run your hands up your legs from the ankles to crotch or up your arms from wrist to shoulder. Each time you do this you will pull a little more of the rubber up and get it closer to where you want it to be. Pull with caution; over time you will begin to get the hang of it. You may want to enlist the help of a friend or fellow rubber pig to help you out. This comes in handy if you have a catsuit that zips up the back.

Once you have it on, gently stretch the arms, legs, tits and crotch to get the rubber properly positioned. Guys, you will have to do the same to get your cock positioned where you want it as well. If you have powdery residue on the outside, a damp cloth will wipe it off.

Now that you have your rubber on, it is time to shine yourself up.

Shining Your Rubber

Once again, there are many schools of thought on how to shine your rubber. There are some people who enjoy the dull color of unpolished latex. Me, I love a shiny rubberman/rubber pig. It is a sign of nasty play to come!

Car care products: A few people like to use car care products. One rubber maker told me he does not recommend *any* car care products. They contain petroleum and other products which could adversely affect the rubber and glue which could shorten the life of your garment. I have never seen a study to verify this, but I prefer to err on the side of caution when it comes to caring for an expensive piece of clothing.

Silicone lube: Many people like to put silicone lube on their rubber to give it a nice shine. Wet Platinum is the most commonly used in my circle of rubber pig friends. Silicone gives you the best shine of any product out there. The downside to silicone lube is it leaves a slippery, sticky residue that easily rubs off on anything or anyone. It is not fun to have a silicone-shined rubber man give a hug to another man dressed in levis or leather. Leather men do not take too kindly to having lube coated on their shirt, chaps or vest. If you wear lubed rubber keep this in mind when hugging or getting close to non-rubbered people. The other downside to silicone lube is that it leaves a permanent coating to all rubber garments. This is bad should you ever tear your rubber and need to repair it. The glues used to repair rubber will not stick to silicone garments, and therefore they are nearly impossible to repair. The only way to remove the silicone coating is to scrub and wash your garment for many hours until it is mostly gone. Even then, you may not be able to repair your damaged garment.

Rubber polish: There are a number of over the counter polishes that work very well to shine your rubber. The most commonly known product is Black Beauty. The polish gives your latex a nice shine. It is easy to apply; simply spray it on the garment and wipe it with a soft, lint-free cloth or, instead of a cloth, just use your hands to spread it around (or get a friend to do it for you - especially on the crotch!). You may want to seek the aid of a friend to do your backside. It can be very difficult to get the small of your back shiny on your own. The downside to latex polishes is that they do not maintain their shine as long as silicone lube. You will need to reapply every two hours or so.

Removing Your Rubber

Many people struggle for fifteen or twenty minutes trying to remove their rubber gear. There is a very easy solution. When you get home, turn on the shower, set it to your preferred temperature and climb in. Allow the water to get under the rubber. The water will work as a natural lubricant, and the rubber will slide right off you. You can also use this as the perfect time to clean any mud, dirt or stains off your rubber. Wipe it clean before taking the rubber off.

Cleaning Your Rubber

As with everything else about rubber care, there are a number of ways to clean your rubber. It is best to wash your rubber every time you wear it. This removes the body oils from the inside and anything nasty you may have gotten on the outside. If you wait too long, you may find that you got something on the rubber that can begin to degrade the rubber and turn it to rubber soup.

The most common method is to wash your rubber in a sink or tub. Most people and websites I visited suggest using a small amount of a mild dish detergent. One site said the detergents can shorten the life of your rubber. I prefer a very mild dish detergent - there is even a product made by Wet Platinum specifically for cleaning items that have lube on them. After you have washed it and rinsed off the detergent, hang it to dry. You can use a wooden hanger if you want, but I prefer to hang it over the shower curtain rod. Every time I walk past the bathroom and breathe in that rubber smell it reminds me of all the nasty, rubbery fun I had the night before.

Make sure to turn it inside out so that all portions of the garment dry completely. Do not worry if you see water stains start to appear. These are normal and will fade as the rubber dries. After the rubber is completely dry, coat the inside of the rubber with talc. You can then hang it in a closet or put it in a plastic bag or box to store.

WARNING: One friend who uses silicone lube told me to NEVER use talc on a silicone-lubed garment. He made the mistake of doing this and ended up with "talc dough balls" on his catsuit that were a real bitch to remove.

L8Xdad suggest washing your rubber with the mild detergent but then rinsing it in another sink that has some Wet Platinum lube in it. He says to swirl the garment in the Platinum/water, turn it inside out and swirl some more. This gives the garment a nice pre-coating of lube and makes it easier for him to put it on and shine. Do not use this procedure if you plan to talc your clothes (see earlier comment).

Storing Your Rubber

There are two ways to store your rubber. Everyone agrees that you should store your rubber in a cool, dry place. Keep it out of direct sunlight and in low humidity. Do not store your rubber next to metal or leather items. These items may contain oils and minerals that can degrade your garment. One person reported storing his leather shirt in a closet next to some leather. A few weeks later he went to get his shirt, and the rubber had come in contact with something on the leather that caused it to begin to break down into a runny, gloppy, rubbery mess. His shirt was ruined.

It is best to store your rubber in a plastic bag or box. You can hang your rubber in a closet; only use wooden hangers. One person said plastic hangers can cause your rubber to begin to rot. Hanging can cause the rubber to stretch and become misshapen. I only hang rubber if I notice the rubber is beginning to get creases in it and I only hang it until the creases are gone.

You want to avoid natural sunlight, as that will cause the rubber to deteriorate faster; white and colored latex can turn ashy if exposed to the Sun's UV-rays. Humid rooms, cellars and basements are not good for latex. High humidity can cause mold and mildew to form on your latex and some of the stains they leave cannot be removed. Do not dry your rubber in any type of dryer, attempt to iron your rubber, or dry clean your rubber. Do not spray cologne or perfume on your rubber. Some of these contain oils that are not good for the rubber. Keep your rubber away from heat sources.

Keep animals away from your rubber. Cats seem to be fond of the smell of rubber. I had a cat that found my bag of stored rubber. He peed on the bag. I now have a pair of latex chaps that have a small, discolored spot thanks to my cat. Other people have told me similar stories about the love affair cats have with rubber.

You can give your latex wear a long life if you follow proper care, cleaning and storage of your clothes. Latex is a love affair for many men and women (and cats). We love to share this fetish and welcome you to our slinky, kinky, erotic fetish.

The authors:

Aqualaboy Paul *is one of the founding members of the Lone Star Rubber Corps, a rubber social club for men in Texas and surrounding regions. He is an avid scuba and deep-sea diver, and works on extraterrestrial projects. He and his mate have their rubber origins as teenagers watching late-night diving movies, and have been wearing their rubber in private and public for more than a decade.*

Alan Stroik *is the founder of the So Cal Rubber Corps, a social group for men who love to live and play in rubber. He is Mr. West Coast Rubber 2005 and a member of Avatar Club Los Angeles. Alan has been active in the leather/fetish/kink community since getting involved with a leather club, the Beer Town Badgers, in his hometown of Milwaukee in the early 1980's. He is happily partnered living in the far flung LA suburbs of San Bernardino County.*

Rubber Videos

Latex videos are a pretty rare commodity when it comes to gay erotica. Since rubber and latexmen are pretty much a small percentage of the fetishist community, most companies go directly to where the most number of people (i.e.: consumers) for BDSM material are. And that would mean leather.

But the number of rubber and latex DVD's has risen greatly during the later part of the nineties and – with the advent of cheap and easy-to-use DVD cameras and software – post 2000. For the most part, and unfortunately, most rubber in gay vids are propwear worn by bunnyclones, the bondage would probably slip off if the bottom would dare to sneeze, the gear merely something cool to wear before you shuck it and get to the sex, and the sooner the better.

Boring.

Thankfully, as latex gear moved more into the spotlight, several prominent companies began making entire segments of kinky movies that actually understood rubber as a fetish. As the Great Uncle of all this, Jack Fritscher, put it, "So many videos say they're going to be a rubber video, and the actor might come in with a rubber coat or vest, but pretty soon it's just flung aside and they're having generic sex. Which isn't very interesting if it's promised to be a rubber-themed video. With Palm Drive, I always tried to layer in more of whatever the theme of the video was."

Fritscher knows the territory. His compilation on Palm Drive Video, *Eight Guys In Gas Masks*, could easily be argued as the first video aimed directly at the rubber fetishist market. He first encountered rubber in WWII, while playing with gas masks. Even at a young age, Fritscher was attracted to the breath control and games you could play with those early gas masks. When he started Palm Drive Video in 1982 as an adult, and released his first set of films in 1984, "I built them around, as I had my photographic sessions with guys, themes. As a writer I knew that editors, if they bought a feature article, were more likely to buy the article if it had photographs to go with it. I would do the triple-play: I'd make a video, shoot the photographs and write an article about it. That was how *Drummer's* rubber issue and Palm Drive were created out of the same incidents."

Eight Guys In Gas Masks was a themed collection of episodes culled from a series of different Palm Drive features. Several of Fritscher's movies would feature men playing out fantasies in a gas mask, even if it may not have been something they'd fetishized about before the shoots began. "It was very interesting to see how these guys were up for anything," Fritscher offered as an explanation as to how he got his participants to pull the masks over their faces. "People would arrive, I'd ask them what fetishes they have and we'd try and work through those. Then I would start adding things on, and if they didn't say no, I'd just keep going, because I like breath control, and gas masks are wonderful for video or YouTube. Gas masks close up breathing, the sound, the breath control. Cigars work so well with them, poppers, dirty socks, jock straps…they found the alteration of reality because it helped mask them from bright lights and the camera; that a gas mask allowed them to become somebody else. They became more alive sexually, erotically, because of the gas mask. What it did as a mask, how it contained their breathing and changed sound, smell and communication in general." In order to make sure at least one new segment appeared, Fritscher added one extra scene. "I shot the last sequence especially for *Eight Guys In Gas Masks*, the one in the football uniform and gas mask." Who was that masked man? None other than Fritscher himself. He freely admits he finds rubber exciting, and was always ready to spread that enthusiasm to his Palm Drive actors. "There is a guy in one of the central features with a big beard and his name is Vigilante, who also appeared in *Drummer*. He'd become so excited during his sequence - by the gas mask - that he came prematurely! He got so carried away that he came without touching himself."

Palm Drive Video offered several rubber-charged videos, including *My Nephew My Lover!*, featuring *Vulcan America* Issue 2 coverman Mike Fritscher; *Mad Doctor*, a rubber-themed movie with a lot of SM and *Pec Stud in Black Rubber*, both featuring Keith Ardent, who was also *Drummer* magazine's first rubberman cover. It took almost a decade before another company found rubber attractive enough to make it a steady feature in their video line, but when they did, it was with a vengeance.

Zeus Studios and Can-Am Productions put a rubberized toe in the water when Can-Am issued *Latex Meltdown* (1995), featuring four latex wrestlers posing, muscle-flexing, wrestling, oil-wrestling, and their rubber one-pieces being torn off. Cast members Marco Rossi, Dallas Taylor, Jimmy Dean and Clayton Titus play out a fantasy of angry models in a cat-fight over who gets the better placement in the photo shoot. They end up spraying petroleum lube on their outfits, weakening them till they can get ripped away from their bodies and the orgy can begin. Photos from that video became the first of many Zeus/Can-Am titles to get featured in *Rubber Rebel* and *Vulcan America*. With *Latex Meltdown*, Can-Am Productions head Ron Sexton made the decision to continue with rubber on his wrestlers, including titles like *Rubber Rumble* and *3-Way Rubber Revenge*, and in the interesting sub-genre of "super-hero erotica," lycra erotica titles through the Hard Heroes company. From the Hard Heroes website: "The ultimate destination for gay super heroes! Imagine tight, hard muscles - wrapped in tight, sexy gear - bound up in tight, vein popping bondage. Or imagine your superhero flexing and straining to be released from some dastardly trap, and then making some evil villain submit to his superior strength."

Zeus Studios head Mikal Bales found the success of *Latex Meltdown* encouraging enough to start incorporating latex into a series of Zeus BDSM videos. As he stated in *Rubber Rebel's* Vol. 4 No. 3, "I believe that if you're going to produce fetish videos, your efforts should be to try and reach every-body." The first Zeus video to approach rubber was *Rubber Roughhouse and Auditions 4*, featuring Kyle Brandon and Brian Dawson, and German musclestud, Wolff. Brandon was dressed in fire engine red rubber to take his abuse from Dawson, and that kind of color was one of the things that attracted Bales. "I'm frequently accused of designer bondage and Hollywood SM any-way," he wryly noted, "so my approach to latex and rubber videos is kind of 'Hollywood Rubber' because I love color! I've always thought that the smell and feel of rubber was primary as far as someone being interested in it, and my company being a visual one, then I would try for color."

Many Zeus models were given their rubber baptisms in Zeus features. Bales recalled that Brandon's initial response to the rubber gear for *Rubber Roughhouse* was hesitancy, but he took to it so well that he wore it to IML (International Mr. Leather) that year. Robert Black, who was honored as Zeusboy of the Year for 1999, was first fitted for rubber while filming Zeus' *Robert Black, Back For More*. For *Vulcan America*'s sixth issue, I asked his reaction to being filmed in rubber as opposed to leather. "I wondered why I'd never worn it before," he told me. "It feels and looks very sexy, very different. It makes you feel naked and clothed, all at the same time. I didn't want to take any of it off."

While many of Zeus' titles became more rubber oriented, The *Fetish Sex Fights* series (four in all) merit special mention. These were issued as Zeus/Can-Am co-productions, and each had serious rubber sequences. In *Fetish Sex Fights One* particularly, Kyle Brandon and Steve Canon began with both men chest-slamming each other while trying to shake the yoke-like bondage that stretched their arms from their shoulders. Once they free themselves, they engage in pulling away each other's hoods, gags and outfits for a winner-fucks-loser wrestling match. The pictures from this video were so hot that Steve Canon's rubber-hooded visage graced the cover *Vulcan America's* debut issue and were part of the magazine's preliminary marketing. *Fetish Sex Fights Two* featured hardbody Mason Flynt and *Vulcan America* Issue 3 coverman Trenton Comeaux in a rip-it-off rubber wrestling segment (and 1998 Zeus Model of the Year Eric Evans in Commando gear!). In the third volume, impressively tall Englishman Spencer Cole and another *Vulcan* Coverman (issue 5), Australian Andrew Lennox, in an International Bondage Rubber Rumble. The fourth in the series featured beautiful, blond, blue-eyed, and nipple-ringed Cody Tyler fucking very sexy Fort Lauderdale muscle-boy Tony Lazzari in a segment titled *Rubber Rough-Up*. The *Fetish Sex Fights* series won multiple Gayvn awards, including "Best Gay Specialty Video" for the first two volumes.

At the time of *Fetish Sex Fights*, the usual black leather dungeon scenes were about all BDSM videos had to offer. It was Bale's decision to go out on a limb that led to something sexier. "I don't think anything fits the body quite like rubber does. I don't think anything makes the body sweat like rubber does. As the body sweats under the rubber, it fits even tighter. That's a very provocative visual. For those people out in jack-off land who can't smell or feel it, I want it to fascinate them."

But Zeus' reputation is in BDSM, and they do have a pair of DVD's that really changed the playing field. *Brute Force* and *Brute Force Two: Expect No Mercy* were two of the most intense BDSM videos to be released in the nineties, and they each featured a rubber-clad Fred Katz doing some serious whipping. International Mr. Leather 1996 Joe Gallagher takes his beating by pulling himself off the floor in a muscularly spectacular fashion, and the moment in *Brute Force Two* when Katz emerges from a warehouse in the woods decked out from head to toe in black rubber is heart-stopping. *Brute Force Two* was also the winner of the 1996 Best Video at the Los Angeles Leather Fetish Community Awards. Getting Katz back in front of a camera (he'd pretty much retired from video work) and into rubber only took a little convincing from Bales, but he did have worries. "It was his idea to wear that rubber suit (in the first *Brute Force*)," Bales told me. "I was concerned, with the way the scene was lit, that we wouldn't see enough of Fred because he would disappear into the shadows. Then it turned out to be fabulous, because he seemed to emerge from shadow as this spectre in rubber from head to toe!

It made the visual all that much stronger."

It was also about this time that I made my first foray into being filmed in rubber. HBO approached Peter Tolos about doing a segment for a new show they were working on called *SexBytes*. Basically a companion to the network's successful *Real Sex* series, they were looking for slightly edgier fare for a separate show. The HBO production crew invaded the *Rubber Rebel* loft in the fall of 1996 and spent an entire day setting up and shooting. There were three couples (one male, one female and one male/female), and me along the side to provide commentary. The segment opened with the seven of us walking along the street in front of the loft, *Magnificent Seven* style, and included one very heavy make-out scene with the straight couple as the two females poured latex across their intertwined bodies. I should also add that Peter and I had one hell of a time cleaning up afterwards. If you recall seeing a gold Buddha answering questions during the program, that was me.

The debut episode of HBO's *SexBytes* first aired in April '97. The liquid latex segment ran about ten minutes as the concluding segment of that first episode. Because of the magic of reruns, it occasionally still shows up. I reprised the gold Buddha appearance as an extra in the movie *The Crow II: City Of Angels*. Although you don't see me, there is a fetish bar scene where the Crow (played by Vincent Perez) pursues Iggy Pop (who plays a murderer known as Curve). I was standing at the bar while all this was going on, even if the camera didn't catch me. But the highest compliment I could have received that day came from Iggy, who took one look at me painted in solid gold and told me "You look like a Greek god." Coming from a god of Rock, that was pretty gratifying.

In the spring of 1999, Mikal Bales approached me about potentially being in a Zeus production. While I am sure he was just being polite (after all, who wouldn't jump at the opportunity to be part of an afternoon where four extremely good looking Zeusmen are strutting their stuff while you're with them?), I modestly agreed. The result was the Can-Am/Zeus co-production *Brutal Kombat*. In it, I got to play Brutux Khan, evil overlord, who entertains himself by having newly captured slaves wrestle and fuck in his presence. With a cast that featured Eric Evans, Robert Black, Beau Bradley and Brent Banes, Mikal essentially offered me what many men only get to dream about. I was garbed in full body black rubber and a pair of bizarre glasses while seated upon a throne for my subjects to be paraded before me. Those men were then ordered to have really hot sex as I looked on, trying to appear above it all. Believe me, trying to be detached while this foursome were going at it may have been the hardest acting gig I've ever taken on. The other trip was when the *Brutal Kombat* DVD version was released, it was my rubber-clad stare that took up half of the DVD menu screen. *Brutal Kombat* became the focal point for *Vulcan America's* sixth issue (the first to appear entirely online) and gave me a listing on the popular Internet Movie Data Base (IMDB.com).

Peter sought to capitalize on the early popularity of *Rubber Rebel* by filming and releasing his own video, *Imprisoned In Rubber,* in 1993. Shot in the backyard of a friend in the San Fernando Valley, *Imprisoned* featured two men, TJ and Lee, who sought to encapsulate Lee in as many layers of rubber as possible. Lee was eventually wearing seven layers of rubber and four hoods, and ended the film double-enclosed within two rubber body-bags. Peter once told me that Lee's hearing was blocked off after the second hood, so directions had to be shouted so loudly that the neighbors were peeking over the fence to see what was going on. Since this was not the normal erotic shoot (the actors were putting outfits on as opposed to taking them off), Peter and TJ explained that they were shooting a video and everything was ok. Unfortunately, after Peter's death the rights to *Imprisoned In Rubber* were lost among legal issues, and this video is no longer available.

Another highly erotic and obscure video came from Scott Baker of Sludgemaster, a club started in Texas in the 90's as The Mudmen. It was released as *Sludgemaster: The Video.* Baker's vision of what qualifies as 'erotic' is way off from the center. The men in *Sludgemaster* have rough sex under the streets of New Orleans, in mudswamps, on oil rigs, or on fields that could be a desert in the middle of nowhere Texas. Four hours of masculine blue-collar men getting it on. These are not models, not porn stars, and they are most certainly not having contrived candy-ass sex. Oil is poured, men's faces are forced underwater till they cry Uncle, a three-way takes place in a sewer, and there is even a wild food-fight-as-orgy scene. Fueled by hard-liquor (there has never been a more erotic tequila worm bitten on film than here) and cigar smoke, *Sludgemaster: The Video* is probably the most outlaw gay movie since the ground-breaking 1972 SM classic *Born To Raise Hell.* According to Baker, it took him almost two years to film and (from an article in *Powerplay* magazine, Issue 7) caused "the breakup of three relationships, numerous brawls in pubs, and was pinpointed as the reason why homosexual men are 'degraded.'" Of course, it is also nearly impossible to find, but trust me, it is 100% worth it.

Somewhere North of Texas, in the redneck backwoods of Missouri, was a different sort of hypermasculine fantasy making it to video. Chip Weichelt founded The Academy Training Center, arranging programs for men who wanted to test themselves against a real prison scenario. Chip hired the best instructors that he could find to work at the Training Center and put his "inmates" to the test. One of those inmates was Jack Fritscher, who had become fascinated by Weichelt's photography that he'd been receiving as advertisements at *Drummer*. "Chip had all these beautiful pictures with all these beautiful guys, and he had this trip going. He was sending in his ad and money to *Drummer* to have his ad published. Finally I said to (*Drummer* editor) Tony DeBlase, 'Are you people fucking insane? You have nothing in here but contest cuties from the Mr. Drummer contest. You have this person here with all this talent and these photographs with this set-up going. It's a pure fantasy! Real cops, SM, gay guys? This should be in the magazine for free!'"

It was with videographer Fritscher's coaching that the earliest Academy videos made it to the market. He told Chip to start editing the security camera footage, and Chip saw the value in this as a way to add revenue. "Chip also figured he could expand on the set décor and the costumes that people were wearing as part of their authenticity into the realm of video, where people could be recruited to come to the Academy and spend money to be a weekend guest," said Fritscher, who can be seen provoking the guards in one of Chip's earliest releases, "or people who were never going to come would spend $39.95 on the video. All he really needed was the encouragement. Chip made some really beautiful stuff." After Fritscher went undercover for *Drummer* at the Academy, he wrote a tell-all feature titled "Incarceration for Pleasure," in *Drummer* Issue 145, December 1990, and remained friends with Weichelt up to Weichelt's death. Chip eventually decided to move the Academy from Missouri to Georgia, telling Fritscher he was making the transition because metropolitan Atlanta would be a better casting pool and would be easier to recruit more and hotter tops who would never come to Missouri.

Chip was primarily into elaborate and gear-intensive bondage performed by a staff that always included real police officers, professional wrestlers, and military. *Force Recon* was filmed entirely in a woods with lots of rope bondage and all in military gear, while two active-duty Marine Drill Instructors tie the wrists and ankles of trainees before throwing them into a swimming pool during *The X-10 Formula*. (And usually, these men were not gay.) He was always on the look-out for new, visual scenes, and was the first man to film a session in a Vac-Rack as part of a video. That scene appeared in *The Collector*. In *Beyond The Law*, a bad cop is kidnapping and torturing victims as other officers on the force try to discover who among them is the killer. One of the restraint sequences is a man cocooned in an inflatable rubber sack while tortured with forced cigar smoke. There was also a lot of diving gear and breath control in Academy features, but in *Academy Training 3*, there is a scene of underwater bondage that few others would have dared to attempt. After Chip passed away in 2003, the rights to his films were acquired by StationHouse Video Distribution, LLC, and they have since been releasing new material found in all the outtakes and deleted scenes that Chip videotaped on DVD. Academy videos are still available and can be purchased through the StationHouse Video Distribution website.

There are still men creative enough to venture into the realm of rubber and gear fetish videos. Two of them are Grey Rose Video and RBR Video. RBR has released three rubber-intensive videos, *Rubber Revenge, Flying High,* and *Endurance.* Producer David Heaton made *Rubber Revenge* in 2002 with an English friend named Lee who happened to be midway between sessions at the Delta and Inferno SM Runs. Heaton views gear in a more practical sense than just as wardrobe. "I have never been all that interested in wearing things, my interest in rubber has been in more functional objects like masks and hoses. I was working with a large company for many years and had a lot of knowledge in desktop publishing and graphics. I had some pretty high-tech equipment at my disposal. So I decided to try to make a video since there didn't seem to be anything out there that addressed my fetishes: those would be medical play, breath control, anesthesia play."

Heaton's studio also has a unique quality about it. "There was an athletic association clubhouse that I decided to renovate into a home, and one of the reasons I chose the place is because it had a large dry basement with an attached bathroom and shower. It looks like a classic-style bungalow from the outside, but it was never used as a home. It was built in '39 as a clubhouse, for men to play poker, drink and smoke in. There was a twelve-foot-long bar in the basement and pool tables upstairs. The showers in the basement were used by generations of young men to shower in after football games, so I'd like to think that a lot of testosterone soaked into the walls."

Shot in his home/studio, RBR's first video shoot took one weekend, the second three days, and the third three days also. Heaton had most of the gear that you see in the videos, but for the third one, *Endurance*, Lee brought most of his own. "These people in my videos exchange being in the videos for play," Heaton explained. When it came time for a more elaborate concept in *Endurance*, inspiration was found in artwork. "*Endurance* is based on an Axel illustration that appeared in Issue Five of *Instigator* magazine that shows three guys suspended in rubber sleepsacks in a dungeon-like area. They're all wearing gasmasks, hoods and other things. I decided to take that concept and expand it into a video."

While the artwork projected a hot fantasy, realizing it took Heaton a fair amount of effort to achieve. "My friend had a sleepsack that had a rear entry, with three zippers in the front: one over the crotch area and one over each nipple. It just happened that, with a person in a leather suspension harness, you could slip it right over them and disassemble the harness and put it back together so that the two front straps are going through the tit holes, and that could be zipped over the harness. Essentially we reproduced the illustration for the video. We put together an impromptu storyline as a medical experiment. How much could he tolerate suspended there all by himself? Then we play out a series of fantasies that he imagines while he's hung there. That shoot took the longest; it is the one I put the most work into. It was about three days to shoot everything and then three solid weeks of editing time."

Slightly less elaborate but just as unique is Grey Rose Video's *Buster's Rubber Romp*. Buster, who was the coverman on *Vulcan America's* fourth issue, is probably the best know purveyor of the population of fetishists who derive their inspiration from balloons. Director Thornton Grey has a rather illustrious resume in addition to his owning Grey Rose Video. Grey was Mr. Drummer 1993 (sponsored by Leather Masters, San Jose and Pleasure Dome), and is on the National Board of the Leather Leadership Conference as a Vice President. He had previously worked with Buster while on the staff of Brush Creek Media, recalling that "Buster was one of the original video stars from Brush Creek. When I was working there Buster had made one video with them, so I directed the next (*Leather Bears At Play*) and put him in it. I started wanting to do movies that really featured him."

Released in 2004, *Buster's Rubber Romp* took a really long time to be filmed. Grey utilized several different locations to get all the participants. "I shot part of it in Toronto and the rest at Russian River (California). The part where Buster is getting off inside the balloon was shot in Toronto. The bonus scene, where he is in a balloon-filled tent with Nate Peirce, was done in Russian River. I wanted to get as many balloons into an enclosed scene as I could, and that just seemed to be the way to do it. I really wanted to cover a lot of bases (in this video). There's a toy scene, and there were a lot of things that we shot that I later decided to take out, like a water sports scene."

In addition to Buster's two balloon scenes, there is plenty of rubber-sex play going on, and Trenton Comeaux is featured getting a coat of liquid latex from Buck Stevens. While some of the actors brought their gear, Grey had to offer alternatives for a few of his Rubber Rompers. "I supplied some of the rubber, because I needed some rubber that was visually appealing. We went to some of the stores in Toronto and they loaned us some gear, and some at Mr. S in San Francisco." He adds, "I was from San Francisco, and you're exposed to so many different things. I liked water sports and that developed into rubber, and then you looked for the best things and kept going."

When I asked Grey which scene was his favorite to shoot, he didn't have to think for long. "Definitely Buster inside the giant balloon. What was so funny about it when we did it was the reaction of everyone else in the room. None of the other guys had seen that before. So everyone from the camera man to Trenton and the actors were just staring! I had to keep reminding them that we were working and to let Buster hang out in his balloon. There's only one Buster. His enjoyment of the balloon fetish is original and unique. There's a sort of trend around balloons but he just makes it special. He really is amazing with his enthusiasm for the work, he never complains and he understands that things don't always go the way you want them. He's not a porn star, he is a guy who enjoys doing what he does, and doesn't have the attitude."

Buster has happy memories from the video shoot as well. "The only thing I could think to mention is how much fun it was to do that shoot. The best part for me was when Austin Masters picked up a big black balloon after I was inside the clear balloon and started blowing it up like mad. He knew exactly what he was doing, driving me over the edge! A big super hot stud in black latex heaving his big chest into an ever growing shiny black balloon! That's what popped my nuts. Too bad it was all off camera."

Buster's Rubber Romp, like so many of the videos described in this chapter, makes its statement by being about a fetish that – while not necessarily out of the mainstream – certainly would not be the first thing most gay men would list as objects of sexual stimulation. It's one of the reasons that rubber and gear videos are each unique to the fetish of their creators and their actors. It also makes them titles that frequently go out of print, the way *Sludgemaster* and *Imprisoned In Rubber* have. My advice for any title you ever see that you may want has been to get them while you can. After all, being able to replay them on your television is vastly preferable to screening them in the memory of your head.

Rubber Personality
Buster the Balloon Guy

Balloons are a fetish for me in the true meaning of the word, being both an obsession and sexual stimulus. However, unlike the psychological definition of fetishism, I don't require balloons to function sexually; they only enhance and further stimulate the experience. The fetish is something that developed as a child and has remained with me as an adult. I have always thought that I was completely alone with this fetish, but in the past few years I have discovered many others that also have balloon fetishes, although most of them prefer to keep it secret and to themselves. Like most fetishes, there are a wide range of activities and images that can be considered arousing with balloons; but for me, the fascination began with the texture and sensation of the feel of the balloon itself, along with the exhilaration of seeing or experiencing a balloon on the edge of bursting.

I like to blow balloons up until they are full and tight and hard and about to burst. At the point when a balloon gets so big that it is over-inflated and pear shaped, my heart begins to race and I find the fear of the balloon exploding an exhilarating rush. Being a bit of an exhibition-ist, I find it a turn-on to show just how big I can blow a balloon myself. Or I press tight balloons against my body, or have tight balloons pressed against my body, against the underside of my genitals in particular. I find the soft, stretchy pressure particularly intense. I also like to lightly brush or have an incredibly tight balloon lightly brushed over my nipples and chest. I like this especially when my nipples are swollen and sensitive.

I like to experiment with different ways of "wearing" balloons. I can pull really big inflated balloons over myself and watch them bounce around, or trap myself inside a huge balloon and then inflate it with an air hose. I like to sit on balloons and see them expand and distort even further; see how much they will take before popping. I like to straddle or lay across a giant balloon while it is inflating and feel it grow beneath me, lifting me off the ground and holding me suspended in mid-air while I hump away against it; fearing it bursting and sending me to the ground.

I love the ringing sound a really big tight balloon will make when you thump it, and the way it wobbles as it bounces. Even the sound of a balloon being powerfully inflated by mouth turns me on. I like to see guys blowing up balloons by mouth. This is especially a turn-on if they are into blowing the balloon really huge, all the way to bursting. I like to watch a rough and tough man touch, play with, or fondle a balloon; particularly if he is not aware of exactly what he is doing. It is kind of a tension of opposites that excites me. I enjoy watching a man pop a balloon, especially if it is as a show of strength or if he's just cocky. I love the smell of balloons....I just love having balloons around, even though they are not always the source of sexual excitement.

I have known that I was a balloon fetishist as long as I can remember. As a child, balloons were my favorite toys. I would always beg for them whenever we were at a store. My step-father would always blow them up for me, but he loved to tease me, and blow them up bigger than I wanted or threaten to burst them. I would squeal in protest, and that only made him blow harder! I was terrified of the balloon bursting, but absolutely fascinated by how big he could blow them up.

Many years later, still fascinated by how big a balloon could get, I tried blowing them that big. The fear/excitement had an unusual effect on me, giving me an erection. At the age of 12 or so I had no idea what was happening, but thought it was neat, so I began rubbing myself with the big balloon. Very shortly afterwards, I had my first orgasm. This reaction only added to my fascination with balloons, and I continued to use them to masturbate with. Of course, I soon also discovered that this was not "acceptable" behavior once my parents discovered my trick. From then on, I kept my balloon activities secret (most kids hid *Playboy* under the mattress; I hid balloons!). I also soon realized that I got the same reaction in my groin whenever I saw guys blowin' up or bustin' balloons. Later in life, I discovered that certain men could produce that reaction even without balloons present, and my sexuality began to take a more "normal" course.

My personal interest in latex wear quite obviously developed from my earlier fetish with latex balloons. The slick texture and shine, as well as the natural aroma of the latex, are stimulants to my senses. I love the way the latex molds tightly to the body, exerting a snug, constant pressure of restraint, yet visually exposing every bump and ripple of the body. I like to wear my latex clothing at the same time I indulge in a session of balloon play, letting the sounds, touch and smell fill my senses. There are also inflatable rubber garments, and groups of fetishists dedicated to that subset of the fetish completely.

Latex is a fetish for a large number of people. Just like leather, much of the appeal of latex is in the tightness and shininess of the material. Clothes made out of latex enhance your awareness of your sensual self, and restraints made out of them can cling like a second skin. There is a definite transformational kinkiness invoked by images of men in latex and rubber gear. Rubber fetish is often associated with open-mindedness and an experimental nature. Rubbermen are turned on by the idea of male transformation with rubber garments and gear and there are many varieties of rubber gear and toys. Latex is a highly refined type of rubber, and garments made of it are usually much thinner and shinier than a rubber garment. While rubberwear is generally made to protect one from the elements and environments, latexwear is designed to enhance the sensations. I still use balloons in a masturbatory manner, and since I have become more open and accepting of my own fetish, have found many exciting ways to incorporate them into sexual play and fantasies with the help of some great fun-loving friends. I am always looking for new and exciting opportunities to explore and promote my own fetish. I have also turned my obsession with balloons into a small Internet business called BigBoys Balloons. BigBoys is an outlet for all different types of large and unusual balloons that I have found the world over.

***Buster** is the stage name of the man who is probably America's best known Balloon Fetishist. He was featured on the cover of **Vulcan America's** fourth issue. He is also the star of several erotic videos, including **Buster's Rubber Romp** from Grey Rose Video.*

A Boner Book

Rubber Publications

Rubber as a fetish in most gay publications took a long time to make a significant impact. In Europe, stories of rubber in kink have been more common than in North America. Magazines like *Toy* from Sweden or *Projet X* from France almost always had a hard-core rubber story in each issue. The French Rubber club, Mecs en Caoutchouc, has a terrific newsletter called *Plan K*, being issued quarterly since the club formed in 1994.

In America, however, rubber as a gay male fetish took a long time to gain a foothold. Perhaps the first time a rubberman graced the cover of a gay erotic US magazine was in *Drummer*. Jack Fritscher was looking for ways to expand the realms of kink. "In 1977, I tried to do an article on rubber as one of the fetishes I was introducing into *Drummer*. I did the first article on Gay Sports, which included some rubberwear, due to the nature of some of the sports. This was before any thought of the Gay Olympics; it was still when gay men and sports didn't belong in the same sentence."

One of Fritscher's first rubber shoots landed in issue 7 of *Man2Man* magazine, in early 1981. Fritscher produced a rubber bondage article with fifteen pictures, including a mummybag. "It was titled 'Leather Hands, Other Intentions,'" he told me. "It was about a 48-hour trip in bondage. There was suspension bondage and head bondage inside a box with an inflatable hood. There was a rubber suit and the man was suspended in a Navy hammock. There's also a picture of a guy totally encased in what, when inflated, looked like a wide hot-water heater with two breathing holes.

"But I wanted to do something more on rubber, so I met with friends of Tony Tavarossi, who was my longtime sex-partner from 1971 to 1981. We went south of Market to interview these guys and they had a big rubber sheet on the bed and they were dressed in full rubber. They said to me, 'to do the interview, you have to be in full rubber, too.' Being a gonzo journalist, I figured I was up for anything. So I got suited up and sat down on the bed, and tried to take notes. But they tried to make everything slip slide away as quickly as possible, because they just wanted to have sex.

"They were two rubber bottoms searching for a top, and I never saw a chance to top that I could pass by. It was freaky and it was interesting and it was new and it was different. That's what rubber was at the time, because leather wasn't enough. I rearranged *Drummer* so it wasn't just about leather. When *Drummer* ran from Los Angeles to San Francisco to escape the cops, it was a leather magazine. Within four months, I had changed it into a masculine-identified magazine, in which masculinity was engineered as a new gender for gay sex, because it wasn't a gender considered available for gay men up until that time. By widening *Drummer* out to homomasculine pursuits, it allowed me to go after things more than just leather."

It was by keeping an eye on what *Drummer's* readers were asking for that lead Fritscher to continue his pursuit of rubber. "What I tried to do was make *Drummer* a verity voice of what the readers wanted," he explained. "I always examined the personal classifieds, because they gave the best survey of what they were interested in. The words most used in *Drummer* classifieds in 25 years were 'masculine' or 'masculinity.' There would be a lone rubber guy here and a lone leatherguy there, so I just worked my way through those things for awhile and came up with these ideas to feature them. Since people hadn't seen this stuff featured before - nobody had shined a light on them – they responded very positively to it. Of course, that recruited other people to them. They could be two different sets of people and keep themselves fresh and happy."

Of interest to Fritscher was not just who was getting photographed, but the photographer himself. His association with the controversial Robert Mapplethorpe began with photos. Fritscher recalled Mapplethorpe's first trip to *Drummer* on, appropriately enough, Halloween 1977. "We hit it off right away and soon became bi-coastal lovers. He had already shot rubber fetish freaks in New York and shared those photographs with me. They were published in *Son of Drummer*, which came out in September, 1978. That was the first time I actually published rubber pictures in *Drummer*. Mapplethorpe was an undiscovered talent with a portfolio; I sent him back to New York and connected him with a couple of people I played with. That's how I designed the cover of *Drummer* Issue 24 for him."

It was the cover of *Drummer* Issue 118, July 1988, that became an historic landmark and produced a rubber icon. Keith Ardent was a porn star who'd been diagnosed with HIV, and one of his dreams, as he described to Fritscher in a letter, was to become a *Drummer* model before he died. "He came here for a Palm Drive video shoot and we hit it off really well. I shot him on a couple of different occasions because we worked so well together, including *Mad Doctor*."

When it came time to create the situation that would become the cover photograph, Fritscher was very deliberate. "I gathered all this rubber stuff that I thought would be of interest to him, to me and to the *Drummer* readers. I purposely went out and shot a *Drummer* cover. I set out to do that, knowing what a *Drummer* cover looked like, having shot eight of them myself over time. I shot this outside; since most *Drummer* covers were shot indoors, I thought that would refresh it. I used lights to light certain parts of the body to make sure where I'd rubbed oil or water into the rubber that it reflected. Since you can't put dick on the cover, I used a piece of tubing around his cock and balls and had it curve around him. I think it is designer without it being at all camp. I left space above his head so that the word *Drummer* could go in without cropping the picture and wouldn't land on his hair or his face or the gasmask on top of his head. And I allowed space on both sides of his body so that titles, authors or photographers could be dropped in without destroying the image in the picture. To me, as a photographer, I like to see the whole picture delivered up to the reader. I don't like to see a picture that might be hot to a reader covered up by all kinds of writing or clipped off by an art designer who is more interested in design than he is about delivering the subtext of the picture. I wanted it to be very rubber, because Keith was a very big man, very built, tall and hung huge. I wanted him to be an aggressive icon on the cover. Passive people don't sell magazines; magazines need tops on the cover to move them. It was framed to be iconic and it suggests all of rubber. Then inside the magazine were all the other rubber photographs that spun out of that shoot."

The *Drummer* photo was a clarion call to rubberists. It paved the way to future issues of *Drummer* and *Mach*, as well as *The Leather Journal's* 18th issue in November of 1990. Featuring a cover of a torso encased in a black and green singlet, it was Editor Dave Rhodes' – who has been publishing *The Leather Journal* since 1987 – first contribution to the world of rubber. "I am into rubber play, rather than wearing it," he told me. "I like getting wrapped up in rubber as tight and as much as possible, to wear it and make me sweat. And I like it for raunch play."

One of the most interesting articles in that issue of *The Leather Journal* was a real-life contribution from Brian Anderson, who was Mr. Vancouver Leather and a member of NWRM. Titled "A Rubber Initiation," Anderson describes the induction of a new friend into their rubber fraternity.

The Leather Journal issue 18 devoted a dozen pages to articles concerning rubber care, where to find gear, an interview with New World Rubbermen founder Bill Bailey, an article concerning Eagle's Shop, a leather store in Tampa, Florida, a write up from London's notorious Backstreet and a twelve-photo rubberman spread. Those twelve pictures, as Rhodes informed me, "I took over a couple year period. I had these pictures, so I figured to make a compilation. Some were taken at IML, some at Living in Leather and other places. There's a picture of Guy Baldwin and one was Bill, who owns a leather store in Florida. I got the photo of him at Fantasy in Omaha." The pictures used in the articles ranged from latex one-pieces to heavy industrial gear, worn by men both in posed shots and at play.

That kind of variety in rubber and gear was the inspiration for Peter "Rubber Bear" Tolos when he launched the groundbreaking first issue of *Rubber Rebel* in May, 1993. In his first editorial, Peter wrote "Seeing men in gear is a passion. Getting into gear is sensuality. Playing in gear is unbelievable sex." While the first issue was a scant twenty pages, it became the first of its kind in the United States. Peter's main purpose behind the magazine was actually to launch a retail business. In a loft in Los Angeles' warehouse district, he'd set up a space to create and sell a variety of rubber and industrial items. The majority of *Rubber Rebel #1* was a sales brochure for Gear Inc., but it also contained the first part of Peter's elaborate erotic fantasy, "Zach." "Zach" would eventually spread over the entirety of *Rubber Rebel's* eight issues.

The second issue of *Rubber Rebel* moved beyond just being a catalog of Gear products to include original drawings and a feature on layering, with photos taken from what would become Gear's first video production. The film was *Imprisoned in Rubber* (which is described in the chapter on rubber video), and became a rubber classic. Peter once told me that "in order to mail it into less permissive areas, we shipped the video with the label *Rubber Technology and Protective Clothing*." It was first offered to the public in *Rubber Rebel's* third issue. That issue also had Peter showing expansion. There was a *Rubber Rebel* party, complete with photos, and an article from the second Mr. Vulcan Contest in Boston, where Peter was a judge and Ryan Johnson the winner. Peter also spelled out his plans for future growth, including a *Rubber Rebel* calendar, the first of his *Rubber Trade* newsletters and the publication of his *Fetasy Guide*, as a resource to businesses that catered to fetish and fantasy. While a catch phrase to *Rubber Trade* was "You Are Not Alone," Peter was creating most of his publications on his own. He began to discover that he had taken on more than he could produce.

With this kind of expansion, Peter needed to take Gear Inc. beyond his one man operation in Los Angeles. While he had plenty of help outside the area from Brian Plant and Daniel Moody, it was a chance dinner invitation to Peter's 1994 Thanksgiving Dinner party that led me to the Rebel's lair.

Rubber Rebel Mascot

We had finished dinner, and he asked me what I did for a living. I told him I'd just returned to Los Angeles from Nashville, where I was working as an editor and layout director for a (now defunct) magazine. Once he discovered that I'd been doing the work on the same Apple computers and in the same programs that he was using for *Rubber Rebel*, he offered me a job. Within two weeks, I'd moved into the loft and began work on *Rubber Rebel 4* and the sixth issue of *Rubber Trade*, and began what became a partnership that lasted until Peter's passing. It was in that *Rubber Trade* that I wrote the first of many articles on rubber, which was my rubber initiation with Peter painting me from top to toe in Liquid Latex, and being led on his leash to LA's Gauntlet II.

Peter, in addition to being a gearhead, was also an artist and tinkerer. The widely popular Liquid Latex was one of his inventions. This excerpt was from an interview with Peter from *Vulcan America's* fifth issue:

VA: You also developed Liquid Latex.

PT: At that time, we were having hoods molded locally in Los Angeles, and I went to the factory where they did it. One of the workers spilled a whole bunch of Latex on them. So I asked about it, its toxicity and other things, and then started experimenting on it. I went to the latex producers and asked them if they could formulate a latex that did not have formaldehyde or other preservatives. What I was attempting to do was develop a latex that had the smallest possible allergenic potential. The latex has to have an ammonia compound, but the ammonia is used to keep the PH high so there's little bacterial growth.

VA: When you got the Liquid Latex idea to fit your specifications, what was the first thing you did with it?

PT: The first thing I ever did was dip my hand into it and make a glove for myself. Then I started seeking out victims! I had someone over for a visit and I was showing him Liquid Latex, and he started dipping his cock and balls in it. Then I started pouring the latex onto his body! First we did it in clear and then in black. Later I got a photographer interested in it and we got two hunky guys in my loft and did a session! And with you, we've made you into a gold Buddha for HBO, and as of this point I've done hundreds of people for magazine shoots, movies and TV shows.

VA: Including (Decathlon Olympic Gold medalist) Dan O'Brien!

PT: A German magazine, just before the last Olympics, wanted to do a photo shoot of Dan O'Brien. They flew us to Idaho where we coated twelve athletes head to toe and Dan from his waist down! The photo was the centerpiece for the Olympic issue of *Stern* magazine that came out in 1996.

VA: You have quite an extensive educational background.

PT: I have a degree in chemistry and biology, which is why I understand rubber and have been able to create rubber fabrics and things of that nature. After that I went to Stanford Medical School for three years and was on the faculty of Stanford for a short time. Later I went back to school and earned two Masters, a Master of Information Science and an MBA from UCLA.

Peter, now free to create gear and seek additional projects, left the creation of *Rubber Rebel* to me. Issue 4 was, in my humble estimation, a classic of male magazines. Peter asked me to create an issue that focused solely on divers and their gear. With two lengthy fantasy stories that concentrated on heavy gear and hundreds of photos, it remains an issue that has yet to be duplicated in intensity. It also chronicled my transformation into the Rubber Buddha. That article is at the end of this chapter.

The response to *Rubber Rebel 4* was phenomenal. It led to a few publishers approaching Peter about selling the rights to the magazine. Before that occurred, we created the mudlarking issue, *Rubber Rebel 5*. While not as well received as the diver issue, it contained one of my favorite stories, the industrial strength "Sewer Rats" (available in the collection of short stories, *Black Gloves White Magic*). Peter was getting increasingly interested in moving into other media about this time. We had contributed to the movies *Se7en*, *The Crow II* and a few television productions, so when the Serengeti Publishing Corporation tendered an offer to buy the rights to *Rubber Rebel*, he said yes.

It was also about this time that Brush Creek Media, home to *International Leatherman* and *Bear* magazines, decided to resurrect the dormant *Powerplay* imprint. Editor Alec Wagner contacted us, and both Peter and I contributed. They used a reprint of my Rubber Buddha article and an original story titled "Inner Tube," viewing the world of rubber kink from one of those truck tire innards. Brush Creek staffer Will Ashton did an in-depth interview with Peter that was headlined "Rub-bear Rebel." In addition to the material that Wagner gathered from us, *Powerplay* Issue 7 (released in August of 1995) contained original gear-intensive photography and video reviews. Dr. Jack Fritscher contributed a cultural anthropological review of Scott Baker's *Sludgemaster: The Video*, which is a classic of its genre.

Rubber Rebel made the transformation to its new owner with a few growing pains. First was the transformation to color, which was a major plus. But it also meant that I no longer had control of the magazine's overall look, and I had frequent arguments with the vanilla art director. *Rubber Trade* newsletter was abandoned, with subscribers folded into *Rebel's*. The fifth (Fireman cover) and sixth (Tom Stice cover) *Rubber Rebels* were pretty good, but it wasn't until the eighth (and final) issue that I got an upper hand in the magazine's layout. Some of the new features that improved the magazine included the introduction of "The Rubber Rogues' Gallery," where I would travel to rubber parties and events and take photo classifieds of attendees, an increased club listing and a greater range of articles concerning non-gear items. It was also in *Rubber Rebel's* sixth issue that my relationship with Can-Am/Zeus took root with a photo-spread from Can-Am's *Latex Meltdown*. That relationship led to my favorite of the *Rubber Rebel* covers, Zeusman of the Year Brad Michaels in silver latex trunks on *Rubber Rebel's* eighth issue. Despite the fact that *Rubber Rebel* appeared to be growing in popularity, business problems at Serengeti Publishing led to the magazine being permanently shut down in December of 1996, even as I had submitted final drafts for the ninth issue.

Since I was now a free agent and Peter was discouraged that *Rebel* had been struck down, he suggested in the fall of 1997 that we attempt to start a new publication. Since he was already well involved in his personal enterprise, Rubber Bear and Company, he secured financing and we christened the new company Butch Media. After tossing around a few titles (including *Gearhead*, *Butchmen* and *Rubber Revolution*), we decided on *Vulcan* (to eventually become *Vulcan America*). The logic was that rubber was vulcanized, there was a Vulcan America Southern California rubber club that Peter was co-founder of, and my friendship with Mikal Bales at Zeus made me think that naming the magazine after the god of the forge was a nice acknowledgment.

So it was that I began work on *Vulcan* issue one. Zeus came through right away with an incredible image of Steve Canon in *Fetish Sex Fights*, rubber-hooded, gagged and defiant, which I excitedly asked Mikal for permission to use as the cover. He agreed and offered several more stills of Canon and Kyle Brandon for the magazine. I had several articles remaining from the aborted ninth issue of *Rubber Rebel*, several of which made it into the first *Vulcan*. Peter contributed a memoriam for a recently-passed rubber buddy.

The last Mr. Vulcan contest and the first Mr. International Rubber contests were written up, along with an interview with Robert "Daddy Bob" Allen concerning his excellent book, *The Wings Of Icarus*. In a matter of weeks, we had delivered our first issue to the printer.

On Valentine's Day 1998, Peter and I stood in the lobby of the North Hollywood post office and affixed four holiday heart swan stamps to each of 250 envelopes before heading off to a celebratory dinner. The response to the magazine overwhelmed us, and we were excited in our belief that this was finally going to make us rich. *Vulcan's* debut met with such a terrific response that contributors began to contact us, along with old friends. Even with that initial success, the second issue was an improvement. I had mastered the use of Quark X-Press for layout purposes, and we purchased some new equipment. With a terrific outdoor cover photograph from Jack Fritscher, *Vulcan America's* second issue was put together. (The name change was necessitated by the discovery of a twinky magazine from the UK also called *Vulcan*.) Mikal also agreed to let me reproduce a gear-intense novella from the Zeus archives called *Sado Island*, with artwork from kink artist Matt. It was, once again, enthusiastically received. A trip to International Mister Leather that year was a chance to really spread the word that rubber was back on the racks. But the magazine headline for IML coverage in *Vulcan America* issue three foreshadowed a coming problem; "IML XX: what's your online name?"

The fourth issue of *Vulcan America* remains my personal favorite. We invited porn star and balloon fetishist Buster to our home for a cover shoot and balloon-sex article. I shot the cover picture of Buster on the carport of our North Hollywood home, while Peter and I set up a fun-filled afternoon of shooting Buster in the bottom of an empty swimming pool filled with balloons. Peter used issue four as the opportunity to debut his design for the Rubber Pride Flag, and there were plenty of photographs. *Vulcan America 4* was where I had set my initial goal with our first subscription offers. The task then became trying to get renewals for the magazine by the time issue five was ready. I was not prepared for what was about to happen.

With issue five of *Vulcan America* underway and issue four at the printer, I was sending out renewal notices. And frighteningly, the responses began to take on a similar tone. "Why should I pay you for what I can get off the internet for free?" In late 1998, the World Wide Web suddenly became my nemesis. Over and over, I heard that refrain as hundreds of wanna-be dot-com porn millionaires began to post their own early websites and expected to become rich in moments (even if they were expecting it to arrive via their Adult Check commissions). *Vulcan America* subscriptions fell by a third. I bit the bullet and, with the help of my friend Bert The Bear, began to prepare a *Vulcan America* website.

Then a greater tragedy occurred. While marketing *Vulcan America* on a trip to San Francisco just prior to the release of *Vulcan America 4*, Peter began complaining of serious pain in his feet. When we got back to Los Angeles, he was rush-admitted to a hospital with a foot infection that was a result of his diabetes. A portion of his foot was amputated that November. As I attempted to complete issue five, Peter's condition worsened. By Christmas his vision had deteriorated to the point that he was declared legally blind, and I was able to get him home-care assistance. I sent issue five to the printer in January of 1999. Peter was scheduled for heart surgery and, as he was being operated on, he died on the table, February 1st. Issue five arrived at the house 10 days later.

Looking back on it now, *Vulcan America 5* was an amazing piece of work created under incredible stress. Another Zeus model, Australian Andrew Lennox flexed his muscle for *Fetish Sex Fights 3* on the cover, along with a strong representation of photos courtesy of Zeus/Can-Am on the inside. Thomas Smith was a glowering image of rubber triumph on the splash page after winning MIR 1999. Fetish gear photographer James Bond had a feature layout, and Larry Townsend had invited me to his massive library for an interview concerning his new book, *A Contagious Evil*. But frankly, I was too devastated to care.

It took a few friends and a major push, and I set out to create *Vulcan America's* sixth issue. *Vulcan America* online had gone live with the fifth issue and I had gone back and posted issue four. Without Peter and the additional revenue from Rubber Bear and Company, the expense involved in turning out a published magazine began to overwhelm me. I had issues six and seven completed, but at that year's MIR in Chicago, I warned some folks that the magazine was in serious trouble and I needed backers if the magazine was to continue. Issue six was already posted online when, in December 1999, three potential backers decided they were not interested in Butch Media. It was then that I concluded - with three month's worth of back bills, a dead automobile and the rent still past due - that I couldn't afford to be doing a fetish business any longer and declared the publication dead. I had to sell off just about everything I had left in order to afford a moving truck and moved to Kentucky to start over.

Once I'd settled in Louisville, another friend, Bob "Zero" Reite, offered to take on *Vulcan America* online as its server. I decided to make the online *Vulcan America* a quarterly photo-zine, focusing on event pictures of men in rubber. Zero posted the magazine I had completed prior to moving away from California, and then I continued taking pictures, writing stories and doing reviews until 2003. It was then that I was offered the opportunity to release my first book, *Black Gloves White Magic* (Nazca Plains) as well as having sold a story to a kink anthology titled *Sacred Exchange* (Blue Moon Press). I began to aggressively promote *Black Gloves*, and a second anthology, *Sgt Vlengles' Revenge* (Nazca Plains), was released later in the same year.

At the end of that year, I took a hard look at my situation. *Vulcan America* (counting published magazines and those created exclusively for the website) had reached its 18th edition. I had recently relocated to Philadelphia to be collared by my Papa Joel and start a new relationship. Promoting *Black Gloves White Magic*, *Sgt Vlengles' Revenge* and working on new material for future books had become a top priority. The original *Vulcan America* website was beginning to look quaint in comparison to more sophisticated web addresses like *The Rubber Lover's Contact List* or *Rubbermen.com*. I contacted Jimmy and Tommy from *Rubbermen* and asked if they would like to archive *Vulcan America* online for historical purposes. They agreed to archive the site and honor existing subscriptions, and on December 10th, 2003, I sent all subscribers to *Vulcan America* online a notice that included the following statement:

*I have certainly enjoyed writing for **Vulcan** and **Rubber Rebel** for over a decade. But the rigors of gathering enough new material to update the website on a regular basis have become secondary to making sure my books get into stores, vending at events, and working up a full-fledged novel. **Vulcan America** has been a huge part of my life for almost six years and it pains me to say that I can no longer keep up with its demands.*

*It's been almost 10 years since I began working on rubber-oriented material for men. I am proud to say that I had a hand in putting our community into a more prominent position than it was back in 1994 when Peter Tolos first painted me jet black with liquid latex and led me into Los Angeles' Gauntlet II bar. No one else was doing anything like **Rubber Rebel** at the time. With the exception of groups like The Five Senses and New World Rubber Men, we were still mostly an underground collective of fetishists. So much has changed since then. Since 1997, Cell Block Chicago has been hosting annual Rubber Blowout Weekends and there has been a growth of interest and attendance every year since. More men from all around the world have been bringing their rubber into the US for a chance to spend a year promoting our favorite pastime. There are more clubs, contests and websites than ever* *before. I don't see the expansion stopping anytime soon, and it's outgrown my ability to cover it as a "hobby." Even with everyone's support, **Vulcan** was never about making a profit, and it never has produced one. At best, it gave me excuses to go to places, visit and have fun.*

With Zero's blessing, *Rubbermen.com* took over the site and posted it until recent governmental issues concerning record-keeping necessitated the removal of photography that was not up to the new governmental code for photo releases (the dreaded article 2257 rules, should you feel like looking them up online).

Rubber publication has pretty much become an online medium since 2000. While *Instigator* magazine has become the vanguard for fetish magazines and certainly includes a large amount of rubber gear in its universe, the internet generation that demands instant JO satisfaction has flocked to the web. Fortunately, there are a lot of fetishists that also happen to be computer savvy. Both *Rubbermen.com* and *The Rubber Lover's Contact List* were hatched from the minds of computer professionals. *Vulcan America 2* featured an interview with Squirm of *The Rubber Lover's Contact List*, who confided that "one of the reasons I started this list was to test software I'd designed at the office."

Squirm was one of the first men to start an open rubber contact list on the internet. An early form of the *Rubber Lover's Contact List* was up in the summer of 1996, and he was also the host of the earliest attempts at *Vulcan America's* website. Squirm's site was connected to the oddly monikered *latexpajamas.com* and eventually became *Rubberlist.com*. When asked why "latexpajamas," Squirm replied, "I originally came up with it as the name for a band. I wanted to start a queer band and sing songs about kinky sex and rubber." In case you were wondering, Squirm is a keyboardist.

Meanwhile, rubberslaves Jimmy B and Tommy DeNial were going full steam with *Rubbermen.com*, featuring hot online video feeds, forums, member contributions and other features that Squirm's site did not offer. *Rubbermen.com* was essentially a monthly rubber magazine with online content, established a few years after Squirm's site. What they were lacking, however, was *Rubberlist's* personal profiles. "We were sharing subscribers and access when it was separately *rubbermen* and *rubberlist*. We made the switchover to the combined *RubberZone.com*." Squirm places the date of the merger in September of 2005. "It was pretty mutual," he explained, "because I had been talking to them for sometime. When I started to re-write the software to make it fully interactive and more of a community site, we realized

– instead of going into competition with each other – why not share in what we already have?"

The newly rechristened *RubberZone.com* is constantly making upgrades. Squirm described future features he is working on, including better chat systems, more streaming videos, and polls for the forums. *RubberZone. com* is part of ShareWeb, and their family of kinky websites includes the robot fetish site *MaleBots*, *Hot4Hogtie*, *BuzzedHard* (for haircut fetishists) and *PupZone*. Much like the old Desmodus family of magazines (which included *Tough Customers* and *Drummer*) or Brush Creek Media's group of publications, ShareWeb offers a variety of editions to explore your individual personal fetish for a new era.

In the last couple of decades, Squirm has personally noticed a great deal of change. While listing *Skin Two* magazine, attending Fetish Balls and seeing movies as his original inspirations, he's happy to see rubber coming more into view in a new century. "When I go into a bar wearing rubber, people are far more engaging about wanting to come up and see it or talk about it. There are still a lot of people that have no clue and talk to you inappropriately. But you don't feel like you're the only person in town anymore. That's primarily because of the internet. In gay media, there's a lot more rubber now. A lot of it is just for looks like leather is often just for looks, but there's a lot more real stuff out there. In print, we have *Instigator* magazine, which I think is doing a lot of great things to show different fetishes and ways to break down barriers. Sometimes – now – you have to go online to find it." And will probably stay that way until someone invents a newer and more immediate delivery system. Until then, Squirm, Jimmy and Tommy are happy to make sure that you find what you're looking for, and get you to understand that, as Peter Tolos informed us on the cover of those *Rubber Trade* newsletters, you are not alone.

From *Rubber Rebel 4*: Building The Buddha

Thanksgiving Day, 1994. I've been invited to the home of the Rubber Bear by a friend who wanted to make sure I would have a decent meal and a pleasant evening after having recently returned to Los Angeles. I hadn't really done anything in rubber before, my sole involvement with the stuff was occasional contact through leather friends. In fact, up to that day, my one individual situation in rubber had been lounging around a friend's house in a fireman's boots and longcoat after asking if he had anything I could wear to keep me warm! The Rubber Bear gave me an early taste of my rubber initiation rites; he opened a jar of black liquid latex and I was cheerfully plunging my digits into it again and again to create a glove cast of my right hand.

A brief aside here. I've been naturally hairless - head to toe - since the age of seven. The condition is known as Alopecia and affects one in 10,000 people. It makes shaving cream and razors alien artifacts to me, and made the prospect of coating me with liquid latex something that Rubber Bear found stronger than anything he could shy away from. No messy preliminary shaving or loose stubble to get in the way. Just soft, smooth skin to smear colors across.

A couple of weeks later, Rubber Bear has asked me to edit the fledgling *Rubber Rebel* family of magazines, and it's his idea to really baptize me into the rubber universe. A quick rearrangement of furniture, some protective plastic across the floor, one steel bowl filled with creamy black liquid latex, me without clothing, Rubber Bear telling me to submerge my cock and balls in a bowl full of the stuff! Well, it was an amazing evening and unfortunately, there were no pictures. We'll end the adventure's descriptions on this note: Rubber Bear produced a pair of boots, a set of tube-type shorts, a collar and leash, and informed me that we were on our way to L.A.'s Gauntlet II for the rest of the evening. After all, what's a work of art if you don't have anyplace to display it? I'll assure you we were the hit of the nighttime world, with even some of my best friends failing to recognize me in my transformed state.

Since that first encounter with liquid latex, I've been turned into a total Rubberman several more times. The best was being the Rubber Buddha, and as you can see from our accompanying photographs, it was hot, sexy, and a bundle of fun. In anticipation of L.A.'s Leatherfest '94, Rubber Bear and I had a trial run for my onstage metamorphosis into the Rubber Buddha. Naturally, being the artist that he is, Rubber Bear had to experiment with shades and thicknesses. For the third time I was going to get encased in a full body coat of liquid latex, except this time our good friend and photographer John Rand was on hand to snap some pictures.

Rubber Bear started with my head, mixing different shades of green with clear (amber) liquid latex in separate containers. He dipped his fingers into the silver bowl once again, and began to turn my bald scalp into the world's ultimate perfect rubber hood. Carefully massaging my head, Rubber Bear began covering my dome, pouring just a little at a time and working the latex into place, moving down my forehead to my brows. He slapped some new color onto my cheeks, guiding the green into place with his fingers and thumbs, pausing only to step back for a moment and smile at his piece of living art. Due to my hairlessness, there was even further he wanted to go, as he began to fingerpaint the lines of my eyes, the sacs below and the nose bridge between. After giving me that first chilling coat...I always get goosebumps!.. Rubber Bear smoothes the green around my skull to get that important first covering. (If you want to do this yourself, a word of warning...I don't have any eyebrows, and neither will you if you get liquid latex in them. Use vegetable oil or Vaseline to avoid the big ouch! Be extra cautious about liquid latex near the eyes themselves.)

From there, we proceeded to coat my crotch, arms, and then legs. In I went, and in a matter of minutes the drying began, a gradual tightening that filled every kink and crinkle of the skin between my legs. Rubber Bear offered me the bowl for seconds, and I willingly lowered my dick and scrotum for a repeat. It felt just as good! I must admit, the sensations are unique to anything that I've ever experienced. A very moist, cool encapsulation, something akin to what an Oreo must feel the first time somebody dunks it in a mug full of milk. On request from Rubber Bear, I took a palm full of the liquid and massaged it over, around and across my groin and the surrounding area. It didn't take much goading from the Rubber Bear to smear my waist and hips with cool, green, liquid latex.

I felt wonderful as Rubber Bear lifted the bowl to my shoulders and let the liquid green cascade off of my chest, down my belly. Something I've quickly learned; liquid latex across the nipples provides an exquisite feeling. The coolness made me shiver, not just with the chill, but with delight from the tingles accompanying my waist and crotch as my earlier dunkings continued to dry. The hardening latex was taking on a shiny luster, mixing with the milk-like coloration of the fresh pourings. Rubber Bear began smearing my hairless ass with more green, giving me the appearance of wearing the most skin-tight of wetsuits. My legs were getting their share of droplets, so they were the next target for full colorization.

Once more, the cool feeling as the creamy fluid poured across the bare skin, then that sensual electricity as we rubbed it smooth across my thighs and calves, watching as the colors deepened through the drying process. We couldn't stop with just the legs, either. Palms full of goo applied to the feet, and don't forget the toes. Seeing how Rubber Bear was trying to be a completist about this, he made sure that the bottoms of my feet were taken care of. (I had to prop myself up on a ladder for this part.) I also had to be careful now; my hands would stick to any part of my body I touched. Not that it slowed Rubber Bear's efforts any. He made sure that any "touching-up" necessary was taken care of. In order to be certain that I wasn't tearing up his work, I positioned my hands upon the ladder to watch as they dried to their more thorough jade, while

Rubber Bear continued to layer the liquid over my body, insuring an adequate thickness.

The latex continued to dry across my body as Rubber Bear continued to build up, thus strengthening, the coats. I could feel every inch of my encasement each time I so much as shrugged my shoulders. Even in my nakedness, I felt as if I were fully clothed, again almost as if someone had wrapped me in a universal wet suit. The constricting feelings as the rubber dried to a uniform tightness, into my pores even, sent sparks up and down my spine, and I can't even begin to describe the sensation of my cock as the rubber followed both its lengthening and diminishing alterations.

Holding up a mirror for the first time, I could see how Rubber Bear had left no space to remain pale. Still, not enough for my rubber sculptor. The Rubber Bear wasn't finished...he took more of the cream and began touching me up again. My ears were pinned to the side of my head with just a touch of latex behind the lobes. My forehead and eyebrow area could use just a dab more coloring with different shades of green, and it never hurts to make that rubber just a little thicker.

In a mere two hours, Rubber Bear had me transformed. After having no more than a passing acquaintance with rubber fantasy activity a couple of months before, I was standing in an artist's studio, as a walking, breathing, sensual work of jade green, marbleized rubber sculpture. There was still one more item on the agenda before Rubber Bear could call me a finished product. He produced a bottle of Armorall and some cloth, and began to spray me down. My skin tight rubber was buffed to an intense, sexy gleam. The first time Rubber Bear covered me, I was scared to touch myself for fear of causing some kind of "run" in the fabric of my containment. Rubber Bear laid that fear to waste soon enough, as he ran his hands (and mine) over areas of my new suit, surprising me with both its fluidity of motion and its strength. Even I couldn't deny the attractiveness of my rubbery reflection.

I wish you could've seen the expression on some of our neighbors' faces when they saw me...a naked little green man...in the hallway of Factory Place! The finale was the pose. I think you can see that our Buddha building was a success. Would you like to rub my belly and make a wish?

Something I'll hint at now is not just how much fun putting on and wearing liquid latex is, but how much of a scene you can create when you're removing it! As you can see from the pictures, Rubber Bear and I had also opened a can or two of black liquid latex and had a sloppy good time with his jeans and shirt; he's so proud of his new pants. I can't get him to stop wearing them. Not that I'd want him to, mind you. They look great.

Rubber Personality
Photographer James Bond

Before I ever knew what "sex" or "gay" was, and when I was about seven or eight years old, I saw a movie that featured a hard-hat diver. He was on a ladder getting ready to go over the side, and they picked up this big helmet and put it over his head, closed the face-plate, and it just took my breath away. It was the most stunning thing I'd ever seen. I started clipping pictures of hard-hat divers. I found them to be a real turn on, even if at the time I wasn't aware of what sex was. It just stayed as a part of my existence; it wasn't my only interest, the way my trains are the driving force in my life. But the diving was always a secret little compartment in my world.

As I got older, it sort of transitioned. Like kids playing cowboys and Indians, I got intrigued with bondage. I never quite related the two initially. As I came of age sexually, the whole thing started to blend together and it formed the fetish. I am an absolute believer in the gay genome, because there was never any question in my life. I had no interest in girls and women, but I was a guy and that was all there was to it. Throughout my entire life, I never questioned that. I never wrestled with my sexuality.

With my other life, you can't do much with *those things* except take pictures. Photography became my real world. I went to the University of Illinois and flunked out of engineering. I was interested in the trains as an art thing, not a mechanical one. That was the 'Sputnik Era' when there was the education gap, so I never had any art courses. I walked through the commercial art department and realized, "that's what I really want to do!" A year later, I entered a two-year commercial photography course. It's the one thing I have been formally trained for as a profession.

It was an off-handed comment like "take a picture, it will last longer" that got me into porn photography. One of the interesting things I found out was that one of the driving forces behind developing photography in France was pornography!

When I was first in photography school, I took the SCUBA course in Milwaukee just so I could wear a wet suit! I had a copy of *Skin Diver* magazine and ordered a $59.99 cheapie custom wet suit, and the first time I put it on, there was no question as to what my reaction was…woof. I remember there was a *National Geographic* when I was sixteen with an article about the sponge divers of Tarpon Springs. There was a line in there that just drove me crazy and gave me wonderful erotic fantasies for the next year: "the oldest diver was 73 and the youngest was 16." The mental image of a 16-year old being put into that diving gear and *forced* to go down into the water was one of the strongest erotic thoughts I'd ever had. And it was more erotic fantasy than any reality, because I didn't know what the reality was. I think a lot of the fetish stuff starts out that way, where the difference between fantasy and reality is sometimes wonderful and sometimes very disappointing. To find someone else interested in diving as a fantasy is still a big kick for me.

There is also a very real sensation, when you're sitting there with all that gear on and the face plate screws into you. And you…*gasp*…*what have I gotten myself into?!?* There's a lot of testosterone running around in that gear. The element of gear with bondage was something that just developed. I don't think I invented it, but I might have popularized it with *Vulcan America*, *Rubber Rebel* and *Bound and Gagged*. Some of the first work I did with B&G was a man in a tight-fitting wetsuit. I thought there was no way I could get into that, but I could get him into it and then tie him up in the wetsuit.

We did a scene with a man from Boston (that became the splash page opening image *VulcanAmerica.com* issue 8). He was in jeans, a fireman's respirator gear, a fireman's hat, hip boots and bare-chested. We had two guys in full hazmat suits looking like they're wrestling him over the open cover of a cesspool. That was over at Valinor farm.

I got Aqualaboy out of the closet on a *Vulcan* article. He asked me if I knew who Todd S might have been. He asked me that name, and there was only one place that name would have come from, and that was in *Vulcan America* (issue 2). Which meant that he read *Vulcan*, because he wouldn't know that name anywhere else. I hinted at it, saying it was some obscure magazine called *Vulcan* that he wrote a story for. Then Aqualaboy dropped it like a hot potato. That was too bad, because Jimmy and Todd had gotten another friend of mine in rubber stuff all hogtied on my hotel-room bed and I was going to take him to my room and say "like this?" Aqualaboy was two doors away, but he wouldn't come out of the closet on that day. A week later I get a phone call from Texas. He's saying, "you know what we were talking about? Well…."

My first in diving suit bondage session was in 1973, in my first apartment in Andover, NJ. A man I contacted through *Latent Image* magazine was the first man I played with. At the time I had a diving helmet and I played with him in the hard-hat. He was totally turned on by that. The element of restraint, like any other tight fitting gear: tight jeans, leather, all very similar with slightly different tactile sensations. The idea of a very heavy, restrictive headgear. We have a number of mutual friends that are into particularly sport bike gear and are also into diving gear. A lot of them will wear rubber diving gear with motorcycle gear over the top. There's a lot of cross-pollination.

I also have one very good friend in my dive group whom I spotted as a gearhead right off the bat. The first time he walked up to me, I saw him looking through the stuff; I thought, "you're a gearhead, you're single, and you're going to stay that way," but we never broached the subject. It took him a little while to come out of the closet, but it turned out he's a furry, the people that are into animal suits. In the dive club, he met another furry! This was an astounding thing for him, because he didn't know any others around. This other furry had a very authentic, perfect bear costume. I photographed it and it looks like a real bear.

Well, he took one look at this costume and he *HAD* to get in it. It's this wonderful thing with this great big head, 48 snaps to fasten it, and he was just in hog heaven. He and the other fellow became very good friends. The other man had gotten a hold of me as James Bond for the diving, so I knew he was kinky, into the gear. A different friend, David, is really withdrawn, but when he gets a costume on, he becomes very animated. When he does dive shows and gets into the demonstration tank, David will get in the water with the dive gear and do the same kind of mime performances that you would do as mime, because you can't speak. They know all the moves and put on a wonderful show. They'd even do the Macarena underwater when that was popular. David sprung a photograph on me that blew me away. He's a nice looking guy with a nice body…and he's got a tiger outfit: paws, tail, massive fierce-looking tiger head; not a comic-book head, but a real one, complete with leather armor that just glistens. I had to tell him that it was some of the kinkiest stuff I'd ever seen from someone who tells me he isn't kinky. But he claims he's not into kink. There is something seething under him that we're too good of friends to just pull it out.

On Kink and Diving Gear

You see the leather fraternity liking tight leathers and form-fitting stuff. You get someone who looks good and put leather on them and it's a major league woof. The same thing goes for rubber and diving gear. One of the prominent lines you'll hear on a dive site is "stand up straight and make the suit look good." We put a mirror in the water, and you should see all the guys that go down in front of that mirror and vent their suit so that it squeezes down on them. You can spot the kinksters right away. The guys who come up in the Dry Suits and don't immediately vent them! A drysuit, when it's squeezed down underwater can be uncomfortable on the surface because it's very tight and just sticks to you like glue. You can tell the gearheads; they're the ones that don't go *pffft* and vent the suit. They'll walk around for hours with their suit all squeezed down. That's a dead giveaway.

By the time somebody gets to me, they're fairly experienced. They know what I am into and the kind of stuff that I do. You have to have a skill set to be able to peddle. I have to say that I have been very happy with the way I've been able to peddle it and absolutely fascinated by the kind of men that have shown up at my doorstep looking to play. I am always pleasantly amazed by the people that offer themselves to me just simply because they know I can tie them up, or put them in gear, or offer some different play stuff for them. The dive gear has been an interesting aspect of it. It doesn't dominate my bondage side. I can play a lot of bondage without the gear, but it adds a little flavor to it. With those who you might not want to pick up in a bar? It covers many ills.

What excites men who can come to me is generally the gear, and the idea of a good top that can tie them up and make them feel good, and they don't have to worry. I am not a threatening image. There are men in the scene that could scare the shit out of you. I have seen this as a characteristic of a lot of leather tops; part of their scene is to be intimidating. The people I play with tend to go the other way. They don't want to be intimidated. There is a big difference between a top and a master. I am not a master, I don't role play; I approach my bottoms one-to-one. It's you and me and I'm here to let you have fun. I will use whatever skills I have to make you feel good. Now, if making you fell good means hanging you upside-down and being unable to breathe for a minute, well, that is your definition of feeling good.

There are a lot of people that come into this, looking at the gear, looking at the scene and all wrapped up in fantasy. When you hit them with hardcore reality, there's a big awakening. The gear may be intimidating but that is the fascinating part. You look at it and go "Oh my god! I'd really like to do that." That is the intriguing part. One of the things I've discovered is a problem is the difference between their fantasy and reality. They don't crank it to the point that says *that hurts*. Well, no shit! When you pull your arms behind you and you pull up on them, it's going to hurt. In your hard-on fantasies, you may think this is the most erotic thing you've ever seen; you do it in real life and you discover you've just disjointed your shoulders. You have to be able to know where the fantasy stops and the reality begins. You don't want to get into a situation where you think somebody could hurt you.

*James Bond got into the kinky photography field when he visited the New York Bondage Club, founded by Bob Wingate, who had an idea for a magazine called **Bound and Gagged**. Bond contributed photos to the very first issue of **B&G**, introducing rubber gear and wetsuits all combined with intense rope bondage. His work has appeared in **B&G, Rubber Rebel, Vulcan America** and on countless websites, feeding the kinky rubber/bondage community.*

A Boner Book

A Boner Book

Rubber Personality
Paul Lewis: Invincible Rubber

Our catalog mails worldwide, to tens of thousands. We're based outside of London. We've had the company now for 14 years. While I was not the founder, at the time I took it we were one of the biggest (gear) companies in the world. I took it in 1992.

A lot of the things we sell are based on personal things that I like, and things weren't available in shops that people were asking for. Like good quality products that don't fall apart at a reasonable price. I designed the rubber police uniforms. I actually had a play scene in San Francisco a few years before that, and it always stuck in my mind that I'd like the idea of that in rubber. If you look at the Invincible catalog or website, you can tell a lot had to do with personal fantasy. Then you design it and see how it goes, and hopefully people will have bought it.

I actually had a real San Francisco cop uniform. It was something I was quite into. Remembering what was on those shirts and then basically coming up with a design. It's not authentic, not any State Police uniform. We call it an American Style Police shirt. Obviously the jeans go with it. When all of the pieces came together for the photoshoot, we rented real police boots, the Sam Browne, we tried to make it look as good as possible. It worked! That image did very well for us and that was a very successful product. It still sells well for us now.

There are ideas that you can work on and improve. You get ideas and you mix them with other ideas, then hope it will sell.

As an Englishman, I believe that since the country is smaller, the concentration is closer together, whereas in the US, which is our biggest market, the audience is so vast that it is spread out. So you see all these people can't come together (like at Mr. International Rubber) all in one go. We sell more rubber to the US than we do in the UK and Europe. I've heard people say that Chicago isn't known for its rubber, but it is! People buy it here! There's loads of places here that sell it; there's House Of Wax, Mephisto's, there's other places. And now with the internet, people don't have to go to Chicago; they can buy it online and have it delivered to their own home. America is so vast that if you gathered all the people who bought rubber in one area, it would be massive.

For what goes into our designs at Invincible, we start with an idea for a design, and then we sample up that product. Say we sample size medium; we'll make sure that the product works and does what it's supposed to do. Then once we're happy with that, we sometimes may have to make two or three prototypes just to make the cut correct. Once we're completely satisfied, we'll put the item into production and get the rest of the sizes made up. When we get the actual item, we'll do the photoshoot (for the catalog) and then market it.

Invincible's products are some of the sturdiest on the market. We use techniques that we have developed over the years, and we use people that have been trained with a background in manufacturing clothing. We have five full-time people in the workshop. We make it all in-house. I want people who know what they're doing. Some of the techniques we use just make the products better; some other companies haven't picked up on that.

We make thousands of garments each year, sell wholesale to shops around the world. Some of the major leading brands that get advertised with someone else's labels - a lot of it is actually made by us. We stopped making the female outfits because the market wasn't as strong. Personally, I thought the men's market needed to improve, so I focused on the menswear because it was something I was more interested in. I think men get a raw deal when it comes to clothing, and especially when it comes to latex. There was hardly anything. I think Invincible made a big difference to men's clothing by introducing the range that we have. We will sell a garment in four of five different colors, so you can choose it in whatever color you want. We offer a custom-made service where a customer can select a t-shirt in the blue instead of the black it's offered in. We do have to be careful. If we start offering too many choices, we'll end up with loads of stock and that would be a nightmare. We have to limit the selections to certain colors that we think would be the best sellers, but there are optional extras should the customer decide to change things.

We spend a lot of time on cuts of stuff to make sure the cut is right. As flattering as it may be, a lot of people copy Invincible designs and cuts. As for quality, I believe in paying money for what it's worth. Custom latex is hand-made and time consuming; the latex sheeting and materials are quite expensive. A customer at the end of the day is paying a lot of money for a garment, and I believe that they should be getting a quality garment each and every time. That is what I believe in. And that wasn't available before we started. People had to put up with what was there, practically thrown together. Invincible guarantees the products we make against faulty workmanship, but we tend to find that we get a lot of repairs from other companies. I could call those companies and say, this is why your articles are breaking, but we repair them. If they're beyond repair, we'll tell them that, too. Our techniques are a little more thoughtful, and that's why our products last longer.

A Boner Book

Rubber Clubs and Organizations

Social clubs have long been a part of the fetish scene, and rubber is no exception. The need to gather and share something so deeply personal is part of the human condition, and the first gay rubber club was organized on December 17, 1964, in New York City, by Elliott Howard and his partner, "Bud" Herr. One of the surviving members of that club, Charlie in Ohio, spoke with me about the early days. As Charlie told me, they began by calling themselves The Five Senses. "We came up with the name because we wanted to use the senses as what brought us to rubber. The touch, the feel, the sight, the tastes and how it sounds when you wear it. Eventually modified to V Senses, this original rubberclub maintained its existence through 1973. "During the (1964-65 New York) World's Fair, there were no gay bars. They were all closed down for the Fair. During that time, we began meeting at a theater on 42'nd street called The Empire. Everybody would gather in the balcony there in their leather and they'd sit together and rub knees. That was your way of connecting. It seems silly now, but that's the way it was.

"After that the bars began to open up. At that time they were gay owned; before, they were syndicate bars. We had one bar before that, on 33'rd and 3'rd Ave, called the Copper Cup. This was the early days of leather. During that time, there was a private club called the Nine Club, which was a leather club that opened that you had to have membership in. It was a bar that you took your own booze into, they had a little kitchen and it was open all night on weekends. Out of that came the association of Band of Pain, which was leather and rubber men."

Weekend trips to a secluded location in Bucks County, Pennsylvania were frequent. "We had guys who owned big summer places in Bucks. One of the founding members had a barn and we converted it. We were professional people and had discretionary income. If it was there and available, the members had it. We would have weekends in the country, and Saturday night after dinner you'd put your name into a hatbox and you would write down who you would want to do something with. If you put your name in the hatbox, you could not reject if your name was drawn. It was always interesting. You didn't have any choice but to go through with it. I did things I never thought I would do, and have never done since those times."

A glossy magazine, *Inner Tube*, was the club's newsletter, and Charlie was deeply involved with its creation. "I was the art editor and did layout. I'd do that work in my office, and we'd would have meetings and put together sessions for the articles." *Inner Tube* was issued three or four times a year and it included hot member photos, original stories, and personal ads. V Senses flourished to the establishment of chapters in London (of which Alan Selby was a founder, and it later became RMC) and San Diego. In 1971, V Senses changed its name to V Senses International.

As happens with many organization, V Senses began to lose steam, and by 1973 had disbanded in the U.S. "It was a very small group, and very private in a sense. Some people never used their names, which was common in those days. In those days, it was first initial, last name," Charlie informed me. "We were never a large club, at most maybe 25 members. We had guys from Boston and maybe Philadelphia. We had meetings at different guys' apartments. You must realize that this group was not a poor bunch of guys. We were a very select, elite group, and there's no other damn way to put it."

Those days were even before the classifieds made significant impact, and Charlie described how rubbermen would track each other. "I moved to New York after college, and I ran into a guy on the bus. He had on a leather jacket and engineering boots. In those days, you wore Levis and engineering boots, and a leather jacket, and that's it. There were no designer rags, and you bought rack. That's how the early days of the leatherbar scene started. Then, eventually places started selling custom. But that never happened in the rubber scene, because we weren't that powerful. I bought my first piece of custom work from a place in London. It was a pair of shorts. Then you would hit second-hand stores, which is where I got my fireman's coat and waders. We were very limited in our outlets for our gear, and I think it was Alan Selby who started making them. Everything came in from Europe, and the quality was not always the best. London's had a very heavy rubber scene for years. Europeans are all together ahead of us in rubber history.

"There was a lot of bonding that wasn't there before. It was the same with the club scene. The club scene was happening about the same time. The bike clubs and leather social clubs were all starting up. I would go to events, like the early IML's, and wear some rubber. You would carry it with you, because you never knew who you might run into. People would come to functions and begin to wear a little rubber, like riding boots, to let you know you had a contact. Or maybe wear a rubber T-shirt under their leather jacket; like wearing clues. It came out of a fetish for the material, and sex was a part of that. Now sex seems to be the essence of rubber. But when the club formed, it was guys who had different approaches, and that's why The Five Senses. It was very sexual, but not like you see online today."

In 1978, several years after the V Senses dissolved in the US, Durk Dehner of the Tom Of Finland Foundation placed an ad in an issue of *The Advocate* expressing interest in locating other men in the San Diego/Los Angeles area for rubber play parties. Surprisingly to Durk, more than just a handful of men responded, and several informal gatherings followed. As rubber fever continued to grow on the West Coast, it was inevitable that a more formal organization would arise. But with his growing involvement in the Foundation, Durk was unable to provide leadership for the group; so the task fell to Bill Bailey. Bill had been involved with the V Senses West chapter in San Diego, and his partner, David Gee, was a member of London's RMC.

Bailey's initial forays into organizing a club came from two inspirations. "While on a trip to England, David and I visited the London Rubberman's Club, which was an off shoot of the V Senses club," he explained to Vulcan America on NWRM's 20th anniversary. "We wondered why we could not get something going in the New World like the Old World. His list of interested guys numbered in excess of 25, many of whom showed up for the first night's get together, which ended up being a fun play party rather than an organization meeting. After this happened, Durk said to me, 'take the list and you organize the group and see how it goes.' Knowing how successful a one man show the original V senses had been, I decided to do the same sort of thing rather than get into a bunch of officers and rules. This was something I had seen in other clubs which caused more hurt feelings than anything else. So the Benevolent Dictatorship of Rubber concept took hold. It was and always has since been to take input from the membership; but since I was expected to do all the work, use or not use suggestions as it fit my needs and ability to get and keep running a club."

In 1979, the New World Rubber Men (NWRM) club was formed. The "New World" designation was intended to distinguish the group from the RMC in the European "Old World." *RubberSheets* was the name chosen for the club newsletter; and though not as polished or glossy as *Inner Tube*, it had the necessary ingredients of hot photos, horny stories, and a listing of club members, along with their specific rubber interests. Bailey did the early newsletters on a manual typewriter. "In the early years I used equipment at work such as copying machines and that caused some nervous moments. In those days, copy places that could handle the 'sensitive material' were not to be had in my neighborhood. *Rubbersheets* was a name that evolved very early in the club's time, and I can not recall using any other name at all. Earliest content was mainly a roster of members wishing to be listed, as the goal we established was to be a rubber contact medium. Sources of rubber gear were also something included in earliest issues."

In 1988, Bailey and Gee moved from San Diego to Port Townsend, Washington, where they sponsored a yearly rubber get together for NWRM members. Bailey's benevolent dictatorship for NWRM proved to be very successful, keeping a group of international men in touch with each other and their rubber. "New World Rubbermen's membership has run as high as nearly 300," Bailey boasts. "I still feel that a place exists for a worldwide rubber contact and information exchange for men in rubber who, for whatever reason, are not using the net. NWRM is truly a labor of Rubber Love, not a business, but a service that I have really enjoyed. The friends I have made through the years are what really made it all worth while." The respect and goodwill that Bailey has earned over the years have carried into recognition from his peers. Bill "Northwind" Houghton gave them the "Aquaward" during Rubbout 8 weekend in recognition of NWRM's 20 years of rubberservice to our community, and a special trophy was presented to Bill as founder of New World Rubber Men for his years of service to the rubber community at the 1997 Mister International Rubber contest in Chicago.

The Boston Leather Knights debuted the Mr. Vulcan Rubber title in 1992 with vanguards of rubber John Ferrari winning the first year and then in 1993, Ryan Johnson (who contributed greatly to *Skin Tight* and this chapter), helping to establish rubber contests in the US. To that end, one of the most influential rubber clubs in America was Men Of Rubber, founded in Chicago by Rich Brooks. They were also host to a *Rubber Rebel* Rogues Gallery and were instrumental in bringing (along with Johnson) the Mister International Rubber contests to Chicago. A newsletter titled *Rubber Pipeline* was issued quarterly with members' information and classifieds. The original MIR logo was created/designed by Steve Zielke. MiR began with social meetings of a handful of men at a downtown Chicago warehouse setting. At one point, membership climbed to over 200 men before the club faded from view around 1999.

1994 saw the formation of the Boston Rubber Club by Wayne Goguen, and Rubber Corps in San Francisco by Tony Sanders. Sanders' Rubber Corps went as far as hosting a *Rubber Rebel* Rubber Rogues party in January 1996. Vulcan America Southern California held frequent parties in Los Angeles and Palm Springs, with founders Peter Tolos and Jim Price opening their homes to activities. Currently, there are several rubberclubs actively operating in the US, including Lone Star Rubber Corps, out of Texas and the southwest; Southern California Rubber Corps just has started out of LA; and West Coast Rubber (home club of the Mr. West Coast Rubber contests in Palm Springs).

There are plenty of active International clubs as well. In France, Mecs En Caoutchouc (Men In Rubber) formed in June 1994. In November 2001, Mecs member Yannick Kerjose won Mister International Rubber 2002, the first European to take the honor. Their club magazine, *Plan K*, is infamous throughout Europe. In Germany, RubClub has begun holding events as feeder contests to MIR, with Michael Schneider, Mr. International Rubber 2006 and Frank Buog, Mr. International Rubber 2005 being RubClub Members. Other illustrious international clubs that have since faded include the Rubbermen of Australia (RMA) and Rubbermen's Club in England (RMC).

A non-rubber club that maintains a high rubber profile is the New York Renegades. They have been hosting the Mister East Coast Rubber contests since 2002. The NYRenegades were also frequent contributors to *Rubber Rebel* and *Vulcan America*, even hosting an early *Rubber Rebel* Rogues Party. Renegades member Nipper organized the first contest at the legendary New York leatherbar, The Lure, with later contests falling to member Dana as organizer. NY Master is a founding member of the Renegades and he told me that the contest came from an idea in 2000, "when the Renegades were talking about what we didn't have in New York that New York could use. The idea came up as a contest…and the idea got put on hold for a few months. Later, we decided we needed something in the fall to kick off the season. We realized that there was only one rubber contest in this hemisphere, that being Mister International Rubber in Chicago. We have a lot of rubbermen that come to our events and runs, so we figured let's try it. Six months later, in the fall of 2002, Mister East Coast Rubber was formed and put on."

The initial contest was enough of a success that the Renegades continued Mr. East Coast Rubber in a variety of venues. Dana, the contest coordinator, claims the hardest part of doing the contest is gathering the prizes. Starting the day after the contests, he's on the computer contacting sponsors and thanking them, and preparing them for the following year. In 2006, the Renegades decided to make the contest into a weekend event.

NY Master, being a longstanding rubberman, recalls getting his first rubber "back when rubber was something that a few kinky people in Europe seemingly did. Just a very few of us over here were doing it, and by then I was already going beyond rubber itself and getting into the various transformations. Like puppy play, rubber ponies and even human furniture, long before the House Of Gord came into existence. That was back when rubber was hard to find and a lot of what you were able to find was the thin, cheap molded stuff that was good for a couple of wearings before it started to tear. Luckily for us, enough of us stuck with it and with *Rubber Rebel* being our poster boy, helping to let other people out there know we were not alone. We started finding out about manufacturers at first in England and Germany."

I asked him what kind of reaction he got when he'd wear rubber to the early Renegades Runs. "Do you think it's gonna rain?" he laughs. "Then they'd ask, 'what do you do in rubber?' My first answer is 'I sweat in it.' I happen to be a traditionalist in that I tend to stick to black, but I really like seeing people wearing all sorts of colors, from yellows to reds, even now the camouflage. Gas masks are very handy with others when I play with others who don't like that I smoke. Or you can do it in reverse when you're into forced smoke scenes. You can control the breathing and even what they breathe." He described one of his favorite gas mask techniques with a pair of masks. "I've got the first one on and my exhalation port is tubed to their inhalation port. They have to rebreathe that way."

Another longstanding rubberman is Bill "Northwind" Houghton. And while not exactly a club, his annual Rubbout events are the hit of many a rubberman's yearly activities. Houghton explained to me the humble origins of Rubbout. "Rubbout actually came together on a kitchen table in Greensboro, North Carolina! I had agreed before taking this trip to NC in Feb., 1992, to do a Rubber 101 Workshop for VASM (Vancouver Activists in S/M), as part of their (then) monthly dinners and demos Sundays. I was also planning to hold one of my usual rubber parties at a friend's out-of-town location.

"Now back in Greensboro, where I was reading my friend's latest copy of *The Leather Journal*. I read the demo listing, with my name there as the demo 'host,' for near the end of March. Hmmm, I think. Interesting. I'm holding a rubber party on the Saturday night before this demo. Gee, all I need is a Meet & Greet Friday night and...*boing!"*

Houghton settled on a name while still trying to put it all together as a full weekend, without having to get sponsorship, dealing with bank accounts, or committees. In an effort to keep the weekend simple, there was to be no registration involved. That way, sudden last-minute attendees could easily be accepted with no hassle. Someone could just show up for any or all of the scheduled events, or a sudden cancellation could happen without loss of a registration fee. The first Rubbout was then held on the weekend of March 27-29, 1992. Houghton recalls the recruitment processes of the early days. "Before there was the public access of internet, I did all my advertising through snail mail mailouts - posting flyers in conjunction with trips I took to the USA and parts of Canada. Mailing flyers to overseas, mailing flyers to anyone who was interested in maybe coming to the weekend. A lot of mailings every new year, just after Christmas. I got buttons made for the first twelve years of Rubbout. Now, dog tags are given out, with different colored edging every year. And there is a price to pay for the weekend now, which includes all ticketed events."

While Rubbout started as a play party styled weekend, Houghton expanded the concept to benefit his favorite community charity. "I turned those first nights' Meet & Greets into fundraiser/raffles for a local charity I supported: A Loving Spoonful, which makes meals for those with HIV or AIDS who cannot cook for themselves. Meet & Greets have gone thru five bars, The PumpJack being the current bar used.

"I organized and ran Rubbouts 1 through 12 (1992-2003) and Rubbout 16 is April (2007). The weekend is starting to get some more attention lately, which I think it rightly deserves. It is the longest-running Rubber Events Weekend in North America, and carries a still low price tag for a great weekend in a city known for its sometimes rain and stormy days in April and for great rubbermen, who wear a lot of industrial gear over their latexwear."

Come time for Rubbout 13, Houghton decided to retire from organizing the event and turn it over to a new person. The responsibility is now, with Houghton's blessing, in the hands of Mitch Kenyon. Kenyon has been involved in rubber for over ten years, attending events with NWRM and as a contestant in the West Coast Rubber contest. After a decade of attending Rubbouts, Kenyon told me how he got to the producer's seat, and about his plans to expand Rubbout. "I went to Bill's place for my first (Rubbout). It's a weekend event, but then it was more of a house party. We tried to take it to the next level and make it into a warehouse, industrial type of party. We've changed focus. It used to be geared to all-sexes-all-types-all-orientations. Now we're primarily gearing to the gay male. We have kept the number of attendees the same, but we are hoping to expand it with more promotion."

While Kenyon has been a rubber contestant, he has no desire to bring a contest into the fold. "Rubbout is unlike many events in that we don't have a contest. It's all fun and sex. No boring speeches, just play. We introduced a slime pit last year and we'll bring that back. We're after sexual energy where people who are new to the scene can socialize and then venture across the threshold and play if they like."

Clubs and events like Rubbout are always a great way to meet people. They provide a safe haven for people to mix, associate, and if the spirit moves them, to play. These gatherings are also ways to lower the level of risk involved from both the health issues (you get to know a guy a little better and reduce the chance of contacting an STD) or of meeting a psycho. After all, there is still safety in numbers. But one of the best reasons overall to attend a club function or event is just to get out and wear your gear. You can find some fantastic energy when interacting with people, something that Kenyon pointed out when he was making his bid to win West Coast Rubber. "One of the things I said to the judges at West Coast Rubber is that rubber is the best of all worlds. It is sort of a fusion between the bear community and the leather community. It has the playfulness of the bear community along with the sexual energy of the leather community." It's why many of us involved in the rubber scene think you're seeing a growing number of people interested in rubber, and why I think clubs and events will continue both to form and to grow.

10 Years of Mister International Rubber

"It put Cell Block on the map as a serious leather fetish bar." - Former Cell Block manager, David Boyer, regarding the history of the Mister International Rubber competitions.

In 2006, The Mister International Rubber competition celebrated its tenth anniversary in Chicago, its host city since its inception. But the roots of that contest go back a fair ways. In 1992, the Boston Leather Knights presented the late John Ferrari with the title of Mr. Vulcan 1993. John was a founder of NLA San Francisco and a charter member of AVATAR Los Angeles. He was also a member of Chicago Hellfire Club, New World Rubbermen and Rainbow MC. John organized the Leather Community Relief Fund to aid those who suffered major damage during San Francisco's 1989 earthquake. The following year, on March 12, 1993, Ryan Johnson traveled from Chicago to take the title from a panel of judges that included John, Peter "Rubber Bear" Tolos, Rick Price, Wayne Goguen, John Paul, Jeff Zirpolo, and John Pendergrast. The Master of Ceremonies for the contest was Michael Smith. There were six contestants for that contest, and a prize package worth $1200.

But then the Mr. Vulcan contest hit a dry patch. Ryan's title as Mr. Vulcan '94 extended to '95 and '96. It was in that year that Ryan and the Boston Leather Knights teamed with the newly formed Men Of Rubber in Chicago and the Cell Block bar to move the contest to the windy city. According to Ryan, "I feared the MVR title was going to fade into just a memory, which was pretty depressing. I promoted the title for nearly three years to keep it alive and relevant, making presentations in New York for the 1994 25th anniversary celebration of Stonewall, several Living in Leather weekends, MAL (Mid Atlantic Leahter) - even in the leather column I authored for the *Windy City Times*. Walking away just wasn't an option. So, I approached the Leather Knights about moving the contest to Chicago, rather than wait for who knows how many years for it to be held in Boston again. Club leadership felt it could be a possibility if a venue could be found and a group to sponsor it. Rich Brooks and I were chatting one night, and the thought of Men of Rubber sponsoring the contest came to us almost simultaneously. Rich approached Cell Block, and (Cell Block owner) Roger Hickey quickly said yes. When I presented the idea to the Leather Knights, they gave their blessing. Rich and I were thrilled. Rich worked on the details with Cell Block and advertising and graphics for the event, while I looked for judges, recruited contestants, and sold advertising space in the program book. It should also be noted that the contest was a fund-raiser for three Chicago AIDS-related charities."

When it came time to bring in people for the first contest, Cell Block manager David Boyer spread his search far and wide. "We looked around at who was in touch with the rubber community, and there was *Rubber Rebel*. We figured we should have this guy because he's in on the scene. If you're going to do a leather contest, there are a lot of guys to pick from for that. But if you're going to have a rubber contest, you're going to want it judged by guys who are into rubber or by guys who have contact with rubber. How could this panel of judges decide which is the best rubberman in the crowd if they weren't rubbermen themselves? There just weren't many people we knew to approach to be judges authoritatively. It was nice when we got to the point where we had enough contests that we could have a panel of judges, and they were all our previous contest winners. Bill Bailey (of New World Rubbermen) and his partner David were always fun to work with as judges.

1996

The Three Mr. Vulcans: L-R John Ferrari, Rich Villagracia, Ryan Johnson

In November of 1996, the first Rubber Blowout Weekend was initiated and Rich Villagracia became the third Mr. Vulcan. Rich had become friends with Ryan several years before entering the contest, claiming that his early defining moment as a Rubberist came from "seeing Ryan at the '94 Folsom Street Fair, being with friends and seeing him on the street in full rubber. Seeing him and going, *oh wow*." When asked if he would be holding the title for multiple years as Ryan did, Rich laughed and replied "No, one year, definitely one year."

Ironically, Rich has held the title ever since, as the following November initiated the start of the Mister International Rubber competitions, but Roger believes Rich was crucial in the early years as an ambassador for the Cell Block's rubber weekends. "For years, Rich was our number one spokesman all around the world. Because he worked for an airline, he was able to visit many places and he made sure that he hyped up the contest and the rubber scene in the United States."

There was also a hostess for the first and only time in the contest, comedienne Carolynne Warren. David found her to be a great host. "She was pretty hilarious. She did a lot of little take offs on rubber items. She reached under her dress and pulled out a rubber chicken. She made these great jokes, she was hysterical." After that, though, comedian Khris Francis became a regular fixture for the coming decade.

1997

Negotiations with the Boston Leather Knights to transfer the title to Chicago did not bear fruit. At that time, Roger and David decided to forge ahead with their own contest and title. When it came time for the name change, Roger noted "We were going to call it International Mister Rubber, but we did not want a conflict with IML. The Powers That Be at International Mr. Leather thought that we'd be pushing it a little bit by calling in IMR. So we turned it around a little bit and everyone was happy with that." Renaming the event Mister International Rubber in 1997, the first weekend at the Cell Block set the blueprint for Rubber Blowout Weekends to come. Play parties, Rubber Brunch at Buddy's (and later, the Kit Kat), and a swap meet. "David originally brought the Rubber Blowout Weekend concept to the table. He felt that we could combine it with several other activities, similar to what IML does. Then maybe do it a little bit better on a much smaller scale. That's where we put together the idea for the Rubber Buddies Brunch, which is held at Buddy's Restaurant, do the prejudging before the contest, and put on the contest with good entertainment and a good MC. (Bar Manager at that time) Patti Brown was a big name in the sash circuit. So a lot of the good advice we got on how to run a contest came from him."

The contest this year was presented by the Men Of Rubber club. There were five contestants this year, and the judges' table was occupied by Bill Bailey, Bill Edmond, Rich Villagracia, Vern Stewart and Joseph Bean. There was also a special trophy presented to Bailey as founder of New World Rubber Men for his years of service to the rubber community.

Rubber Blowout Weekend 1997 was not without some conflict, however. Across town at Man's Country that year, International Mister Leather sponsored a Mister World Rubber contest on Sunday the eighth; the day after the first Mr. International Rubber contest took place at the Cell Block Saturday the seventh! Keith Waltrip went home that year with the one and only Mister World Rubber sash, and Christof Lerner became the first Mister International Rubber. The MIR '98 first runner up that year was Walt Waskawicz and second runner up was Michael Vayinger. Christof, a native German, was calling Lexington, KY home at the time. David Boyer remembers Christof as one of the bigger surprise winners of MIR history, because "Christof was in Chicago for the weekend and we actually talked him into entering the contest. We were like 'Be in the contest…who knows, you might win. You're here, you might as well enter…' as opposed to having a couple of guys already with their gear and ready to go."

Keith Waltrip, like many rubbermen coming into their fetish in the 80's, credited seeing fellow Chicagoan Ryan Johnson as an initial inspiration to engage in rubber as a fetish. When interviewed for *Vulcan America's* third issue (at IML 20), he stated that seeing Ryan "at the Chicago Eagle, when he was encased in black rubber…I just couldn't stop touching him!" Mister World Rubber was quietly tabled after that one year.

1998

In 1998, the irony of Thomas Smith accepting his sash from Christof was in the fact that the title would not be venturing all that far. Like Christof, Thomas was a citizen of Lexington Ky. Or at least, a close association. "In fact, I lived in Minneapolis, Minnesota," Thomas informed me. "I could say something like I had a close connection to Lexington, Kentucky, since I had been Mr. Kentucky Leather 1997 and resided part-time in Lexington, Kentucky and Minneapolis, Minnesota." First runner-up that year was Michael Ryan from

Cincinnati, Ohio, and second was Stephen Krause from Munich, Germany. Scott from Sludgemaster was on hand that year, and his infamous videos were played to the delight of those in attendance.

When interviewed by Dave Rhodes of *The Leather Journal*, Thomas had strong thoughts on the contest and its future. He said to Dave, "I have traveled to London, Amsterdam, Australia and across the country; I have observed a large interest in the rubber fetish. If you look at the Rubber Lover's Chat List or the Rubbermen web sites, it is clear that there are lots of rubbermen."

This was also the first year that the contest included a live onstage "shower scene" as part of the competition. Inspiration for the shower came from David Boyer. He recalls, "The first year we did the contest as Mr. Vulcan Rubber, we required contestants to perform a fantasy scene. Nobody wanted to do that. They were like 'I want to be in the contest but I don't want to play out a fantasy onstage.' So we nixed that, realizing that other contests were going at the time, what could we put in the show that would be entertaining and people could play around with, have some fun, and get a little sexual without being a fantasy set-up? That was when I thought, how about if we hose them down? The biggest complication at that time was we were talking about running water on a floor that isn't a bathroom, where there's no floor drain. So how do we build something that retains water until we can get it out of there? Then it was 'how do we get the water to come down?' The first year we started, we built a water tower, and had them stand under the tower. Khris would have to turn a little knob on the back of the tower that would start the water running. It got pretty wet and sloppy, but it was a lot of fun." With this new feature becoming a fixture, Rubber Blowout Weekend prepared to march into the next millennium.

1999

"Can you believe we're alive to say this? MISTER INTERNATIONAL RUBBER 2000!"

It was with those words that Comedian (and regular Rubber Blowout Weekend MC) Khris Francis introduced the winner of the next year's title, Tom Kelly. The first runner-up was Bruce "BD" Chambers and second was Jim Drew. Kelly took to traveling after winning the title, and making friends both for and in rubber. "I went to most of the events in the US and one in Berlin. Titleholders weren't a big deal in Europe at the time. Here in the US, I went to MAL and met a lot of neat people. I met people like Jon Krongaard, who introduced me to a lot of IML people and other people in the leather community. He encouraged me to go to the Leather Archives and Museum opening."

The growth in just one year of the rubber scene was evident: from the demos to the preparedness and desires of this year's five contestants to the expanded Saturday swap meet and vendor fair. This was also the year that Mister International Rubber went webwide, with a live webcast of the contest via the Rubbermen.com site. Kelly felt that this kind of growth expanded as each MIR year continued. "The contest created visibility for rubber in the US. And now with both East Coast Rubber and West Coast Rubber, we have them going as well. Whether the contest itself creates visibility or the side-effects create the visibility, there's still more visibility for rubber. That's the good thing."

Mother Nature was at her most co-operative that year. The weather was so mild that many in attendance shunned cabs and jackets to walk in the warm Indian Summer-like conditions. With the weekend's temperatures rarely falling lower than the 50's during the day, and nary a drop of rain (or winter snowflake) in sight, a few of the package ticket holders arrived for the regular Buddies Saturday brunch in T-shirts!

There was plenty of hot rubber in every variety. Sexy stylish suits mingled with men in full hardcore gear. There was a liquid latex demo covering the bodies of the curious, giving the Cell Block a delicious smell of rubber from the moment the lights opened on the contest. The panel of judges was composed of Mr. International Rubber 1999 Thomas Smith, Mr. Vulcan Rubber 1997 Rich Villagracia, NWRM founder Bill Bailey, *The Leather Journal* Publisher Dave Rhodes, and myself.

2000

The following November, when I boarded my flight to Chicago On November 10th, 2000, I was taking a seat as a run-of-the-mill tourist, prepared for a weekend of rubbery fun and maybe some debauchery. I was attending this year's Mister International Rubber contest as a citizen and not as a judge, since one of the attractions of the fifth anniversary of the Rubber Blowout Weekend that year was to have four of the five previous winners returning as judges. As far as I was concerned, this was more time for me to horse around, see friends and behave like a working stiff!

So imagine my surprise when, as I entered the Friday Night Welcoming

Party at the Cell Block, Manager David Boyer met me at the door with a big cheery welcome and then proceeded to ask me "How would you like to party on us?" It seemed that Mr. Vulcan Rubber 1997 Rich Villagracia had been called off to work at the very last minute and a stand-in judge was required... and so for the fourth time I was being seated as a contest judge. Not that I objected! The judging panel for the year's contest included the remaining rubber titleholders selected from the first four contests. Joining me was Mr. International Rubber 2000 Tom Kelly; Thomas Smith, Mr. International Rubber 1999; Christof Lehner Mr. International Rubber 1998; and rounding out the judges' panel was Dave Rhodes of the *The Leather Journal*.

This was, without exaggeration, Cell Block's biggest Rubber BlowOut weekend yet. The biggest crowd of attendees, the largest turnout for contestants, the hottest swap meet and vendor area...you couldn't help but get excited by all the rubber contact to be made that year. When returning host (fresh from a Lake Tahoe gig) Khris Francis began his evil comedic rants for the third year, and the final judgment turned the title over to this year's winner Chad McLaughlin, you just couldn't help but get swept up in the excitement. Tommy DeNial was first runner-up, and Jim Drew, second for the second year in a row.

2001

The contest hit several new highs this year, the most important being that this year's winner was truly the first International Mr. International Rubberman, as he traveled all the way from Paris to Chicago. Yannick Kerjose boarded the plane back to France with the 2002 Mr. International Rubber sash in his luggage. Second-place contestant Jeff Detweiler hailed from Seattle, and Californian James Miller was the final runner-up from a field of seven. There was the usual sea of friendly faces uniting for what had become for many of us, a regular autumn pilgrimage to the Cell Block bar. There were a couple of new faces at the judges' table as well. Durk Dehner of the Tom Of Finland foundation, and Bob Maddox, the founder of Male Hide Leathers of Chicago, joined this year to sort through the field of applicants. We had a new host this year, as well. Jeff Roscoe added a welcome different touch to his guest emcee duties, including his skills as a singer and songwriter. (And his fabulous flippers!)

I recall the moment I knew we had a winner on our hands (from an audience point of view), when Yannick came out during the shower exposition, with his boot pre-filled with water and dancing sensually for the crowd. Up till then I really felt everyone was running neck and neck. But everyone had their special moments...especially "Uncle Dick" from Ohio, whose fantasy description was a standout!

There was another standout moment that had nothing to do with the competition. Michel Roupert, the publisher of France's rubber magazine *Plan K*, made an impassioned speech about the feeling his French Brethren have towards the citizens of the United States after 9-11, and then presented the Leather Archives and Museum with a complete set of *Plan K* magazines, courtesy of the M.E.C. (Mecs en Caoutchouc - Men In Rubber) rubber club. It was a spine-tingling moment, and when Yannick was announced the winner at the closing of the contest, you could feel the pride in the room.

An important aspect to having a winner form overseas is that we could claim as fact that Mr. International Rubber was now an even more broad-based competition. With Yannick being able to get to more of Europe than any winner before, the opportunity for other rubbermen to become aware of the competition increased the opportunities for more rubbermen to visit and build upon what the Cell Block and its staff and management had been supporting since 1997. Roger viewed Yannick's win as a turning point in legitimizing MIR. "When Yannick won," he explained, "I was very glad about that. I wanted it to be a legitimate title and not just a bar title."

2002

Seven men were ready to vie for the title, a new stage setting laid out to make the event take place in a locker room (complete with shower), and the return of the always acerbic Khris Francis to provide bite. By the time Mr. International Rubber 2002 Yannick Kerjose came on stage to give his farewell speech, I doubt if anyone in the crowd knew who would be donning the new title, but it was Chicagoan William "Rubber Willi" Schendel who stood front and center to accept the sash at night's end. Willi has since become one of the driving figures in keeping the contest progressing forward. "Willi has traveled all over the world. He is very much into the rubber scene, he knows the people to contact, and he's a dynamite guy to work with. He just took hold of the contest and ran with it," is how Roger views it. "My parting words to the new owners of the title were, 'It would be a good idea if you if you treated Rubber Willi very nicely, because he can do you a lot of good'."

Willi decided from the very start to use the title as a means to bring more men into the MIR circle. "I saw IML as a venue to get to the interna-tional crowd while they're in Chicago. A few years ago at IML I started something I called The Rubber Agenda, which is a separate set of rubber events that correspond to the IML schedule. That way rubber guys have something to do while they're there and they don't have to hang around the leather guys the entire time, but they can have something that's just rubber guys. There is a play party that is in the Agenda. I worked with Worldsites and with Master Mike Zuhl (of International LeatherSir/Leatherboy) and hosted the first Recon party. I just tried to find as many ways as I could to meet people." Willi also saw IML as a means to reach the international attendants that come to Chicago "The Mr. Rubber Italia contest that happened in 2003 happened because they had come to IML and found that there was Mister International Rubber. They said if there was MIR they needed to send someone. The very first Mr. Rubber Italia was Pannucci Andrea: he finished second at MIR (the following year)."

The 2003 first runner-up John Reddy of Alexandria, Virginia, and second runner-up was Elmar Koeller of Marpingen, Germany.

2003

In the year that Mr. International Rubber 2004 was won by Las Vegas' Chris Vincent, there were a lot of changes being made. Roger Hickey had decided to sell the Cell Block, and this year's Rubber Blowout weekend was also meant to be an introduction to the two new owners. Unfortunately, the new occupants were woefully ignorant about what a fetish bar was, and basically ran the bar into a ditch. Even to the point that, as David put it, "I was fired the following weekend. I didn't even get to send thank you letters to the participants." By the following April, Roger had taken back control of the bar. While Roger, David and other bar employees had kept many records and photographs of the MIR contests, Roger was soon to discover that almost all these documents had been destroyed in the few months in which the bar had changed ownership. While the less said the better about the two men left unnamed here, all parties interviewed for this chapter described the duo mostly in epithets. Both Runners-up this year were international contestants. Mr. Rubber Italy, Pannucci Andrea was first and David Peachey from Sydney, Australia, was second.

2004

The loss of much of the general information led to several challenges for Willi and the way the contest was organized. "I started taking on the responsibilities for MIR in 2004. I jumped in behind the scenes for Mr. International Rubber 2005. I worked really closely with Jeff Roscoe. He was helping the bar get back on its feet. He was the man who created the MIR website. I had to come up with a new application. My goal became to get all the basic questions out of the way. When I entered the contest (in 2002), the application was one page. Now the application is three pages. We ask questions like, what are your club affiliations? What do you think is a distinguishing characteristic of rubber? It's a little more in depth and that gives the judges a better idea of who the contestant is and where they can probe further."

Frank "Bug" Buog from Otterstadt, Germany, headed the first international sweep at the Mr. International Rubber 2005 Contest at the Cell Block in Chicago, IL on Saturday night, November 13, in front of over 200 cheering spectators. Frank was also the man to hold the first ever Mr RubClub title, Germany's newly-founded gay men's rubber contest. David McLay from Montreal, Canada, was first runner-up and "Rubber Matt" Matthew Grevink from Sydney, Australia, was second runner-up. Nine men competed from all over the globe. The expansion of contestants and contests was something that made Roger proud. "When there are contests like Mr. East Coast Rubber or the Palm Springs contest, that's when you realize that you've really done something. They had a series of elimination contests in Europe for a representative to send to Chicago for Mister Rubber. The man from Australia was a real coup."

The judges were Mr. International Rubber 2003 Rubberwilli (head judge), 1999 Thomas Smith, 2000 Tom Kelly, 2001 Chad McLaughlin, and *The Leather Journal's* Dave Rhodes. Khris Francis emceed with his spicy brand of humor which, as usual, took no prisoners.

Mister International Rubber Contestants in 2005: L-R Heindorf, Winner Michael Schneider, Runner-Up Alan Stroik, and Aqualaboy Paul

2005

For only the third time in the run of the contest, a new Master of Ceremonies ventured forth to host the ninth Rubber Blow-out Weekend. Jinx Titanic played fast and loose with the crowd, getting more and more wild as the evening continued, along with ASL interpreting by Brooke MacNamara. Michael Schneider, Mr. Rubclub 2005, was elected as Mr. International Rubber 2006, the second German in a row to win. (Counting Christof in 1997, the third German overall.) Alan Stroik from Southern California was present as Mr. West Coast Rubber, and placed as 1st Runner-Up. Also competing were Paul Shank from Houston and Kevin Heindorf from Chicago, who stole the show with the memorable catch phrase "Fuck you like the bitch you wanna be."

Michael is not just a rubberman, he is also a Saint...sort of. "I am a member of the Sisters of Perpetual Indulgence," he informed me. "I am not a fully-professed Sister, but I am a Saint. I am not Saint Michael, but I am known as Saint Phoenix. I am not allowed to do some actions on my own; I need a fully professed member beside me, either a Sister or a Goddess." On his own, Michael used his title as a method of spreading the good word about rubber across Europe. "After winning MIR, I attended several contests in the leather scene in Germany as a judge, and a rubber contest in Rome, Berlin for Folsom Street Fair, gay prides in Paris, Zurich, Nuremberg, Munich, London, Europride, and Vienna for the LifeBall Charity Event benefit for HIV/AIDS." He also has one other accolade to be known for: Michael is also passionate about sport dancing! He was the German champion 2005 in Latin formation dancing.

Judges for the contest were Mr. International Rubber 2005 Frank Buog, Laura Petriella of Vex Clothing, Bill Stadt of the International Mr. Leather organization, Tommy DeNial of RubberZone.com, and Chuck Windemuth of the Chicago Kennel Club (a titleholder grooming organization). This was a change that Willi was aiming for. "We wanted to get out of a rut of having the previous winners always being the judges. All the previous winners were saying they wanted to relax and enjoy the contest, so we pushed to find judges that were not previous title holders except the one stepping down. We needed to begin to cultivate and find out who are the people who are worthy or need to be judging this: you have the credentials, the experience, you know what we're looking for, would you be our judges."

As occurred at the contest of 2003, Roger Hickey used the occasion to announce that the Cell Block would once again be changing hands and introduced a new owner. But this time, the signature belonged to an experienced leather bar owner, Frank Blondale, who had officially signed the papers on August 31, 2005. While Frank, as owner of The Detroit Eagle, had a good idea about the mores of a leather bar, the rubber contests were new territory. He told me, "At that time, pretty much nothing had been done for the Mr. International Rubber 2006 contest. I wasn't aware of how little had been done or how much needed to be done. Thank God RubberWilli was there and was active on the part of the contest. That was what got us through the first year. Willi knew that something was stirring, and that there was going to be a sale (of the Cell Block); so as soon as Roger and I signed the papers, Willi was in touch with me."

The circumstances of that first contact were unusual. "I was on my way out to judge Mr. West Coast Rubber for their first contest," Willi recalls. "As I was on my way out, I called Frank and introduced myself. It was the first time I ever talked to him. I said 'By the way, these guys are doing this contest that will be a feeder contest to MIR, I need your permission to give them gift certificates to send their winner to our contest. It would be good publicity.' The first conversation I ever had with him, and I was standing on the El Platform getting ready to go to the Mr. West Coast Rubber contest, asking Frank's permission to give away gift certificates over Labor Day Weekend."

"I had not been to an MIR before," said Frank about his newness to MIR. "Obviously with (The Detroit Eagle) my weekends are spent in Detroit. Detroit is kind of unusual in that we don't even have a gay leather shop here. There is one leather store, but it is basically straight. As far as a rubber vendor in the Detroit area, there isn't anything. Most guys in Detroit either go to Chicago or Toronto for leather gear. Toronto has a really good store that has a lot of rubber stock."

With the ownership of both the Cell Block and the contest still in a re-organizing stage, details on and registration for the weekend were not available until around the start of October. Under the guidance of Mr. International Rubber 2003 RubberWilli, small revisions to the format were made, judges were empanelled, and a great contest weekend went down. David Boyer, like Frank Blondale, gives RubberWilli a lion's share of credit for keeping the contest alive. "He took up the torch," David says. "He was a good ambassador to begin with. After he won the title and I was still there (working for Cell Block), he was going out to these places, like a party or a club weekend, and getting people excited about being part of the whole thing."

2006

As Mister International Rubber approached the tenth year, Frank and RubberWilli decided to attempt to make the contest grow. Frank began laying down groundwork for expansion, starting with venue. "I had a meeting with the folks at Circuit (a club) in Chicago," he informed me a few months ahead of the 2006 contest. "We got them settled as the contest venue for the tenth anniversary. We had a lot of discussion about having a change of venue for the contest to Circuit. I'd been listening to other people, and part of the idea is that MIR, if it is going to be seen as something besides a bar contest, needs to have a little bit of distance from the bar. We had taken a look at theaters and other places like that, and the problem is they were either too small or way too big. Ultimately what you want is slightly packed – not too many people to be uncomfortable, but more than enough people to fill it. You can't have a 500 seat theater with 200 people or it looks like nobody came! Circuit was accessible to the bar and the host hotel."

With the contest expanded to a two night show, it was Mr. Rubber Italia 2005 Maurizio flying home with the title. First runner-up was Frenchman Eric from Paris, and from Canada, Frank from Montreal finished as second runner-up. The expanded contest included an opening contest Shower Competition at the Cell Block on Saturday night, then the final contest taking place on Sunday afternoon at the Circuit Club. There were additional categories for scoring this year, including a first-ever audience vote. Maurizio had stepped down from his Mr. Rubber Italia title just before coming to Chicago to take home the MIR sash. Judges for the contest were Hervé Bernard, Mr. International Drummer 1998; Roger Hickey, former owner of Cell Block and Mr. International Rubber; Ryan Johnson, Mr. Vulcan Rubber 1994; Fred Katz, former owner of DV8 NYC and Zeus video actor; and Michael Schneider, Mr. International Rubber 2006.

The 2006 host was Eddie Hibbs, aka Sister Erotica Psychotica of the Los Angeles Sisters of Perpetual Indulgence. "The main reason I had Eddie come this year," Willi explained, "was I had people saying about previous MC's that they demean the contest or don't give it the respect it deserves. I thought 'Ok, we're going to have a Nun!' Nobody's going to argue with a Nun. And Eddie's really in the scene, knows what it's about, understands it, has rubber gear and wears it. He was also great on stage and kept the contest moving."

With the Mister International Rubber contest and the rubber weekends set to move into a second decade, all the principals from the past and the future see MIR as an ongoing concern. Even if the new owner of the title, Frank, claims, "I don't know where the future of rubber is in the US. I know that it is a major mover in Europe. It's interesting that the leather scene is kind of fading. I am not sure there is going to be a scene to replace it. Leather 30 years ago was kind of a catch-all. If you were into anything fetish, you went to a leather bar and you wore leather. Then you did handkerchiefs and signaled what particular fetish you were into. Things are more broken down today. I think that folks that are into rubber or bondage or fisting or piss or whatever it happens to be are saying, 'I'm not going to buy a bunch of leather to walk into someplace, because I'm not into leather. I'm into rubber or fisting or whatever.' I don't know if any particular fetish will become as big as leather once was or still seems to hold sway. On the other hand, I think rubber will be a major player. It is interesting, because I thought about where MIR might be in five or ten years. But I think the contest will remain viable over that time."

As for maintaining the vitality of MIR, Willi is ready for the challenge. "It's my baby," he emaphatically states. "It is something I am very committed to, for better or for worse. When I entered the contest, in my interview, I said I wanted to help grow this contest. I wanted to help it become more viable and to bring the reputation of the contest up. One of the things MIR has going for it is that it's small enough that you get to know people. And I think it's still focused on the fetish. I think if it gets too large, it becomes commercialized and too much of something else. I would like to see it land somewhere between where we are now and where Mid Atlantic Leather (MAL, a yearly leather event held in Washington, DC) is." He also wanted to add an important kudo to the newer tone of the contest's look. "Ron Volanti and Jackie Weinberg are also two really important people. Ron does all the photography for MIR and he's one of the three official IML photographers, and Jackie does our graphic design. So we do a photoshoot, then I give them to Jackie. I give her concepts and she comes up with a logo. This year, I asked her for fire. I was thinking of a torch or flames; she came up with the flaming swirl for 2006."

There was also a personal touch that Roger believes gave MIR (and other Cell Block sponsored-events) a personal touch. "Early on, *Rubber Rebel* magazine gave the support we needed to keep this contest going. You're a big lynchpin in that," he told me. "We were family. Whenever we had these events, whether it was a leather event in February or a rubber event in November, we would take the contestants, judges and their spouses to a nice restaurant, and treat everybody well. We know that if we treat our guests well, they'll treat our audience and our contestants very well."

Being able to keep the contest at the kind of family level is something Willi echoes. "I always tell the judges you start judging Friday as soon as they get their numbers. You watch the contestants and see if they're moving around the room, are they talking to other people, are they sticking with their clique. When someone comes up to them, did they shut them down really quickly? The guys who think they're God's Gift to rubber aren't going to win this. We've had really hot guys who come into this contest, who get on the stage thinking, 'I'm the hottest guy on the stage and I'm going to win this,' but they're complete assholes. It's not all about looks, it's not a beauty contest. I take very seriously that the person who wins MIR is an International title holder and they need to be the International representative."

When I asked Roger about the recognition that the contest has given rubber in both the US and around the world, Roger declared, "We didn't realize we were doing it at the time, but that's what happened. Back in the first year, we saw that there was certainly an interest in that fetish, certainly participants in it that came out of the woodwork that first year when we promoted it. That's when I thought it would be a good idea if we kept it at any price. It was kind of natural because Chicago is already on the map in the leather community because of IML. IML has been a gathering of the leather clan for more that 25 years. So it wasn't hard to do. We had the people already interested in coming, we were known internationally in the gay/fetish community, very big in the leather community throughout Europe. I think when people saw there was a rubber contest being done in Chicago, they thought they could travel here and give it a try. Then they were pleased when they did, even if we never made money on that damn title. Almost every dime that came in went back out in the area of promotion! The business itself was promoting the thing, with full color flyers and trooping all over the world. If I put everything together, I could tell you that there was no money made. The last two years we were there, I think we managed to cover our expenses and maybe recoup maybe a thousand or two thousand dollars, and that was it. But over the years, I have been very excited by the people that I have met and that have participated in this contest. Although everybody's gone into it with their eyes open, they all wanted to be winners. Very seldom did I run into any resentment for any of the runners-up or people that didn't place. For the most part our contestants have been very congenial, very collegial; I think they had a lot of fun doing it. It's taken on a family reunion quality."

David Boyer echoes many of the same sentiments. "I had the idea that the contest would grow into something when we started it," he recalls. "My job has always been to show people a good time. I think everyone of the guys that has won the contest has been good for the contest. I think they were good title holders; they were fun guys to work with. I always enjoyed bringing everybody together; to see people come from halfway around the world, from one side of the country to the other, and from Europe or Australia, and hug each other....it was a homecoming of a sort for them. Just being able to provide that made me feel great. That's what I really enjoyed doing."

The Rubber Pride Flag

Many communities in the fetish scene have developed their own special variance of a "pride flag," and the Rubber Pride Flag has been in existence since 1994. Developed by Peter Tolos and Scott Moats, it has since made its way to t-shirts and lapel pins and, of course flags, among other items. There is some dispute as to how exactly the flag was originated, but the main event did take place at a Vulcan America Southern California Rubber party.

Peter felt that this symbolic flag could be a way of identifying ourselves as rubberists to one another. When Scott and Peter discussed a rubber flag on a Palm Springs patio during a rubber get together, they worked on a concept, and then drew up the design which was modified as the group made suggestions. To Scott's recollection, "I designed the main look of the flag, Peter drew it up at a Vulcan America meeting while I was standing over him describing what I had in mind. Peter put in his ideas, such as the coloration."

Peter claimed the he'd had the idea for a flag for five or six years, before the actual creation of the first flag took place at that 1994 event. In an interview from *Vulcan America's* fourth issue, he stated, "I was hosting a Rubber Party in Palm Springs. We were talking about making a flag, so I drew up the basic design. Then Scott Moats (Rubber Knights of San Diego) and I modified it and I did the final drawings of what the flag is now. To me it's a nice way to identify similar, like-minded men.

"I looked at the other flags that are around, like the Bear Flag and the Leather Flag, and I just wanted something that would be more distinctive. There are very few black flags, so the basic color is black. But it also needed some bright areas, so the red and the yellow were used. Basically the yellow originally was for water sports and the red had to do with blood, but I've interpreted it slightly differently since. The little 'V' that's in there stood for Vulcan, which was the Rubber Club that had started and indicated a kink. Rather than have straight bars across, it has a kink into the flag and that makes its intent fairly clear, then cheerfully added, "it's a kinky flag!"

At the time, Peter considered that there was no real rubber community and little support for Rubber activities. There were a few groups, not necessarily clubs, dotted around the country, but they lacked a way to find like-minded people. "Only a few people attended events; relatively few people supported *Vulcan America*, and attempts to stir up interest in rubber clubs were disappointing. Finding other rubbermen, especially in the US, is difficult because few rubbermen ever go out in gear. As a group, gays, and especially fetishists, remain under attack, so any effort to get us together can only help us to fend off such incursions into our freedom to be free-thinking adults. Promulgating that symbol helps to develop community." Since then, the internet has provided a way for not only rubberists, but all fetishes, to find their way out of the closet. One of Peter's main rallying statements was "You are not alone," which aided many in coming out and not being afraid of their desire for rubber.

Scott also viewed the creation of the flag as a uniting symbol. "I wanted to give something to the rubber community; I believe it should be free for all rubberists to hang with pride and unity. I have a rubber copy of the flag and use it often. It is still my desire to see it used freely within the community."

The ownership of the image was signed over to Peter by Scott on January 31st, 1998. At the time, it allowed Scott to use the flag for any way Scott saw fit in San Diego, and stipulated that all other uses were to be licensed through Peter. Upon Peter's death, it was Peter's request that the flag's image be allowed to enter the public domain. He really desired the flag to float free for whoever wanted to use its image.

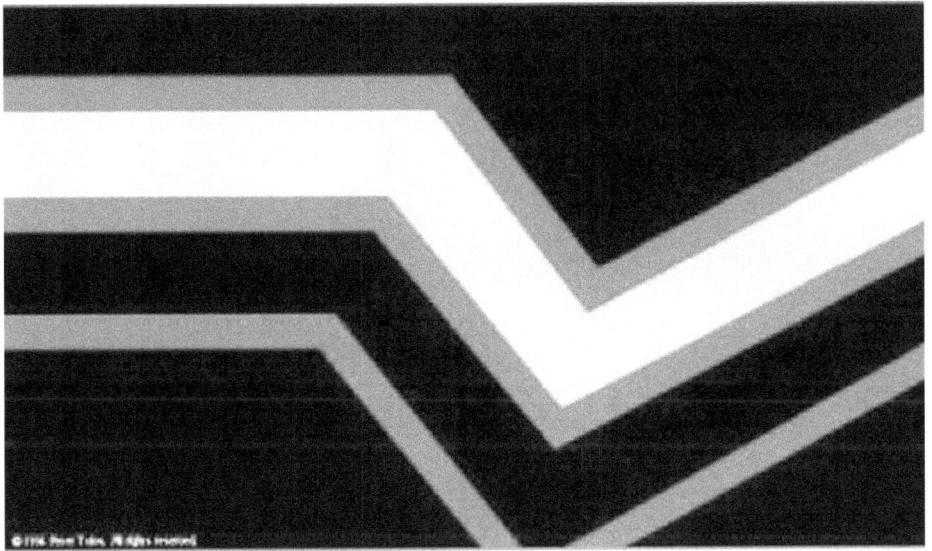

Rubber Flag

A Boner Book

Fiction: Zach by Peter Tolos

The ad really turned Zach on and revved his fantasy dreams. He read the ad again......

RUBBER DADDY BEAR
Looking for muscular body builder son interested in learning about Rubber Service. Tattoos a +. Total encapsulation, gas masks, bondage in rubber and leather. Come for a weekend, stay for a lifetime.
#1685

...and then he called.

It was time to meet Rubber Daddy Bear. Naturally, Zach was nervous. While he loved leather gear, his only experience with rubber was when he wore a rubber t-shirt for a posing session. He liked the feel and got rock hard, fantasizing often after that about wearing rubber pants, rubber hoods, of being bound and gagged in rubber.

Every time he thought about it he got a raging hard on, even a couple of times at work. He couldn't control it. Once he saw a guy in rubber in a bar and creamed right there, but he was too shy to talk to the guy.

Now, here he was, driving to a stranger's house for a weekend in rubber. Exciting thoughts, worrisome concerns. He had never given himself over to another person, trusting him with his sexuality, having control over his life. But the talk with Jack was soothing yet exciting at the same time, talk of encasement, bondage, breath control, enclosed in layers of rubber and leather.

He was ordered to appear in full leather covering his heavily muscled body, and he had it on the leather - T-shirt under his leather shirt and motorcycle jacket, the cod-piece leather pants and chaps, which protected his beautiful round ass even further than usual, and emphasized his basket. Heavy Wesco engineer boots and a motorcycle cap rounded out his leather outfit. And there was the hood he had to wear just before he rang the bell. He followed his instructions and came to a nondescript bungalow.

He walks to the door and pulls on his mask, as the musky leather smell invades his lungs. Adjusting the mask, he laces it tightly, puts on his gloves, makes out the doorbell location just before he zips the eyeholes and mouth shut. He presses the button.

Brrrinnng.

Then silence. He stands, hoping he hasn't gone to the wrong house. He waits, visualizing a little old lady opening the door, then screaming and dying right there. He waits. Maybe it would be a ten-year-old looking dumbfounded at this six-foot-two asshole standing there enclosed in leather, a shining black specter. Maybe...a sound. He waits, less sure he wanted to be there. A creak. Was that the door?

A hand grabs his neck and pulls him inside. He stumbles sprawling to the floor.

"Get up! Asshole!"

He starts to rise, but the pressure on his shoulders keeps him from rising full length.

"On your knees, shithead."

He obeys as he feels the man come close, pushing his head into his Master's crotch. Then he smells the man and his rubber. Taking it all in a deep breath, his cock stiffens in its leather cage, twisting as it straightens in his leather pouch.

He smells latex as his zippered mouth is opened. He sticks his tongue through the mask lips, tasting the rubber crotch. Taking the fullness of the latex into his mouth, zach finds the Master's rod and licks through the rubber, making it grow and harden. He sucks on it and it becomes warmer and he longs to take it in his mouth.

"Open the flap, cunt," the voice softened.

zach finds the flap and sucks the hard dick till it comes through the opening. He licks it, tastes it covered with rubber and takes it in his mouth through his leather hood, sucking it and abrading it with his teeth. And it grows and hardens, the rubbered shaft moving over his tongue, into his throat, lubricated with his mouth juices as it slides deeper. His breath, shut off; his mind consumed with the smell of his Master, with wanting to please. This was what he wanted to do, what he wanted to be, how he wanted to feel.

Suddenly the Master withdrew his cock. Had he done something wrong?

zach was slammed on the shoulder and lost his balance, falling sideways. He heard nothing and lay there confused. Then some steps and his Master's voice close to his ear, "Take off your clothes. NOW!" he roared.

zach complies, hurriedly taking his boots off, unsnapping, unzipping his chaps, pulling off his pants, jacket and struggling to pull the leather t-shirt over his hood. He begins to undo the lacing of the hood and a hand stops him. "Not yet, fuckhead...stand up so your Master can whip your naked ass."
He does. He knows his smooth, almost hairless body glistens with his sweat, showing off his tattoos. He hopes he is pleasing his Master.

Slap! Ouch! He jumps as he is swatted on the ass, again, then another. The man has studded gloves on. He feels his skin reddening as his Master slaps his thighs, his stomach, his chest. The man hugs him and kneads his back with the studs. He wants to cry out, but he won't as he is held tightly in the man's bear hug. He smells rubbing alcohol and this man coats his body with it, stinging the welts, yet soothing and cooling his red skin.

His Master unlaces the hood and pulls it off. Fresh air. But just for a moment. "Put this on, cunt face."

It was a rubber hood, tight fitting and stretchy with mouth and nose holes. He cannot see. A finger probes zach's ass, and a large dildo is slipped in, hurting for a moment.

He is handed a rubber outfit and told to put it on. He sits and does as he is told. One piece. Pulling it over his feet, he feels the coldness; smoothing it over his legs, he feels it warming. Hands grasp the inside of the outfit, sliding it over his stomach. His hands are guided into the arms, and the heavy latex catsuit snaps over the shoulders, holding tight to the body, stretching over his muscles, clinging to his skin, merging with it. His cock and balls slide into a lubricated rubber sheath, stimulating him and making him hard. It feels so good. zach squirms and wants to yell out. He has never felt anything like this before.

The zipper is closed. zach feels gloves being pulled over his hands and he pushes into them up to his shoulders. Gauntlets are snapped over his wrists, and the neck of the hood is put under the suit. He feels the dildo being driven deeper into him as a full rubber harness is put on, being tightened and adjusted.

A thick collar of heavy rubber is locked on zach's neck, tight. Then cuffs are buckled to wrists and ankles.

Now he is totally encased, encapsulated in shimmering, black rubber. He is RUBBERMAN. Anonymous, dehumanized. There is no man here, only a slick, muscled rubber body. He is energized, this vision in black.

His sweat trickles down his tight suit onto his legs. He feels great, oozing pride at how he must look, thinking of a glistening rubbered body, enhancing his muscles, showing off their bulk. zach stands proud, tensing his muscles and he knows his Master is staring at him, lusting for him. In turn, he lusts for the touch of his Master.

He is led roughly to another space. Chains are clamped to arm and leg cuffs, the collar and harness. Clanking chains are tightened, pulling on his arms. zach is lifted off the floor swinging, a black rubber puppet controlled by heavy metal. The RUBBERMAN is made to dance in the air. He rises and hands pull him forward by the ass as a hot mouth surrounds and sucks on his rubbered cock.

zach shivers as he squeezes the dildo deep into his ass, and his Master's mouth massages his cock in its lubricated sheath. he moans and he hears his Master grunting, slurping like a pig that is eating him, pulling and twisting his rubber cock. A vibrator now goes to work on his groin, it is pressed against his ass making the dildo vibrate deep inside him. He feels it, he loves it. Now his balls are vibrated, he twists and shakes with elation. Pressure builds. zach can't control it. No, not yet! Not yet!

"AHHHHHEEEEI!!" zach cums.

His Master holds him tight as he writhes in his rubber ecstasy, dangling from the chains. he shivers and twitches. The cum squeezes in his tight rubber sheath, oozing over his balls, warm. zach cums again, and the hot cum is forced into his crotch, burning, into the skin.

His Master drops him slowly down to the floor, cuddling his rubber boy. zach feels the strong arms around his waist, massaging his shoulders, his butt. His Master plasters his mouth against his boy's rubber face and he caresses his boy's rubber cocooned head. zach's tongue shows pink through the mouth of the mask, and his Master sucks it into his. They kiss and suck long and deep, twisting their tongues, each filling the mouth of the other. zach grasps his Master in his rubber arms and feels his Master's rubber, the chains, still attached to his wrists, clanking, reminding him of his confining encasement, of where he wants to be, of where he is.

zach feels his Master cumming, he becomes briefly rigid before his ecstasy, before exploding, and then the masculine shout of joy, the heavy breathing, the shaking, the utter thrill of having another man with you, reaching the soul of lust, the touch and release of rubber sex, the mystery of complete enclosure, the encasement, the security. zach loves this rubber world, he loves this rubber man.

The rubber hood is torn off and sees his rubber prison, the gas masks and belts lining the walls, the heavy rubber suits hanging empty from the walls. zach knows they will be filled with him soon. Suddenly, his Master blindfolds his eyes and whispers, "Rest now, boy, we'll do more later." The chains clank to the ground and zach is led to a rubber-sheeted bed where the two lie together on rubber.

He smells the rubber pillows and sheets, he smells the rubber Master he hasn't seen yet, he smells his rubber world, and dreaming about a rubber tomorrow, he dozes.

He dozes, he dreams....
Our rubberlad is in bed with his Rubber Dad, comfortable in his rubber gear with rubber smells permeating his very being. He floats, dreaming a rubber dream......

...the last thing I wanted to do was to go to a costume party. I hated costume parties. "Why did every overweight closet queen decide that a costume party was their only chance to 'come out'?" I thought to myself. "I'm only going because Ron insisted...Ron is really wearing thin. Now I have to go rent a costume.

"This could be worse than the party itself. I'll probably get stuck between a Prince Valiant in pink tights or a giant white bunny."

Dave, the bartender at The Hunter Bar, listened patiently as I moaned and groaned on and on about the entire situation. "Listen," Dave finally said, "A friend of mine runs a small costume shop. His stuff is kind of interesting - a little on the unusual side."

"Well, Hell," I thought, "any friend of Dave's."

I'd wanted to get Dave alone for a long time, 6' tall, muscular, and lean with dark hair, a full beard, and nice furry buns, or so I'd been told. I'd also been told that he was into some pretty weird stuff, which sort of intrigued me while making me a bit nervous about approaching him. "Tell him Dave sent you," he said as he handed me directions.

As I approached the building that looked more like an abandoned warehouse than a costume shop, I went up the front steps onto an old loading dock and up to a door with a small hand-painted sign. The Costume Den, Walk In. I did. There was no one at the old, beat up, wooden counter, so I rang the bell. I nearly came right there as he walked through the swinging door from the back room. Just under 6 feet, broad built, shaved head with a coarse, dark goatee, his muscular hairy chest stretched the tank top he wore. He had what looked like a black rubber wristband on his left wrist that accentuated his muscular forearm. His tight faded jeans strained at the crotch with what must have been a huge cock. That's where my eyes were lingering when he finally asked, "Can I help you?"

I rolled my tongue back in my mouth, explained what I was looking for, and that Dave had sent me. "It sounds like you might be interested in my special collection. By the way, my name's Max," he said as he shook my hand. "Come on, the collection is in back." Taking me through the swinging door and through a maze of dark hallways, we finally came to a locked steel door.

He put in the key, turned it, and ushered me into a room that was empty except for an old set of metal closets and a long mirror.

Max went to a metal closet and clanked the door open, revealing the outfit. I couldn't believe my eyes when he pulled it out! "I can't wear that to a party, it's...well, it's...anatomically correct, sort of."

Sort of was only the half of it. It had a long, thick, pliable cock that was covered with a row of long spikes up the top and around the head with huge low hangers the size of tennis balls. They looked like they should have been attached to a Klingon, but they were attached to this bizarre one-piece latex suit.

The head looked like a bull, with long horns and thick flowing hair embedded in the latex. The hair continued under the chin and down the center of the impossibly muscular chest. The hair also ran down the neck and the center of the back, narrowing as it approached the thick shapely butt. There were tufts of hair on the shoulders, at the crotch, and on the tops of the feet and the back of the hands.

The entire beast was muscular from its thick neck to its clawed feet and hands.

"Hell. you can always put clothes on it if you want to take it out for the evening," joked Max. "It looks hot in a black leather jacket."

"Yeah, I can imagine shoving that cock and those balls into my Levis", I replied.

"Well," Max said, "you have to try it on to really appreciate it."

"Why not?" I found myself saying.

I stripped down. Max opened the zipper that ran from head to waist down the back and pulled out a bottle of lubricant from his closet.

"What's that for?"

"The cock and balls can be kind of a tight squeeze," he replied as he lubricated the inside of the suit and handed me the bottle. I lubed, getting hard and wishing

Max would help. He handed me the suit with instructions to start feet first.

I pulled the suit over my feet. It was surprisingly soft and slippery, having been dusted with a fine powder. As I pulled it up to my waist, Max went to work reaching into the suit and working the cock and balls through what felt like a rigid ring, and then working just the head of the cock, and then my balls, through two other rings.

Max then pulled out a hex wrench and inserted it into a small hole under the balls and I could feel the cock ring built into the suit tightening around my cock and balls, as he continued sealing my privates into the costume.

"Don't want anything out of place," Max said as he tightened the ring around the balls and the one that held the head of my cock inside the thick, spiked, head of the suit's cock. I was really getting hard by this time, and as I did, the tube covering my cock telescoped out and grew with me.

I stood and Max eased the suit over my ass, helped me slip it over my arms and shoulders and finally my head. The suit tightened around my waist and chest. Soft, warm rubber totally encasing me as he zipped it up slowly, being careful not to catch the hair that covered the zipper flap.

I'd never felt anything like this, it hugged me so close it almost hurt. The eye holes and mouth lined up. With his guidance, I rose full height and he turned me towards the mirror.

I started when I saw what I had become, this huge, hairy, muscle bound-alien. I could see my cock expand as I stood there, and I could feel what must have been the weights inside the balls pulling down.

"Why don't we try on a few accessories," suggested Max, as he opened wide the second closet. It was filled with all sorts of black rubber gear.

He started with a heavy, black, full rubber harness. Before he fastened the strap that ran under my ass, he lubricated a large black butt plug and slipped it in through a slit in the suit I hadn't noticed before. The tight black harness forced the plug all the way in and firmly in place. He then laced a pair of long black rubber gauntlets to my forearms. I looked at myself. I was unbelievable.

Max grabbed me roughly and pulled me to him. He stuck his tongue through the mouth hole and I passionately sucked on it. He put his hand on my shoulders and pushed me to my knees. He slowly unbuttoned his Levis and pulled out his meat. It was larger than I had imagined.

He grabbed my head, shoved his cock into my rubber covered face and started pumping my mouth on it. I sucked it in through my rubber lips, swallowed it as deeply as I could, gasping for air when possible.

Finally, he pulled back and said, "Now it's time for some real fun." He rummaged through his closet and came out with a heavy rubber collar which he strapped tightly around my thick hairy neck. Then wrist and ankle restraints, proportioned for my beastly muscular limbs, tightly sealing me further into my rubber prison. Finally, he pulled out a huge black gas mask with dangling rubber tubes. He slipped it over my head; the lenses had been painted black.

I heard the clink of metal as I was backed up against the wall, secured spread eagle and left there chained to the wall, enclosed in total rubber darkness, and sealed into a rubber, muscular, alien prison.

Some time later, I heard two people come into the room. I jumped as the whip cracked across my cock, causing it to grow in anticipation. After working my cock over, they unchained me and then re-secured me on my knees, with my head down and my ass up in the air.

The harness strap was unbuckled, and the butt plug was torn from my ass to be quickly replaced by Max's cock. I could hear him grunting as he plowed my ass with his huge man meat. He finally swore as he filled my ass with his cum. I was about to relax as another cock, larger than the first, filled my hole and started pumping hard and fast. We exploded together.

I was untied and lifted to my knees. As they tore the gas mask off my face, I found myself kneeling before two muscular men dressed identically from head to foot in shimmering, slick black rubber. Both stared at me through huge alien eyes. The slighter man pulled off his hood and said, "See, I told you this place would have what you need."
"Yes, Dave," I stammered, "I mean, yes, Sir, this is exactly what I need."

Dave gently kissed my snout as Max pulled a bottle and a small plastic bag from the closet. "And we're going to keep you like this for a long time," said Max, as he ran glue down the zipper, being careful to keep the hair out as he sealed down the flap.

Dave replaced the butt plug and harness, and then inserted a balloon catheter. He remarked, "By the way, you're going to be a real hit at that costume party."

He woke and for a moment and saw in the closet a rubber costume with a bull's head. His cock sprang stiff. He stirs. He wakes...

zach is now awake from his dream.

He almost feels the heavy rubber costume in his dream, his balls ache where the costume's gigantic dick held his own dick in a steel ring built into the beast's cock and balls. He can feel where his costumed Master turned the wrench and captured his cock and balls.

His hair tingles at the image of being sealed into the suit when the Costume Master ran cement over the zipper, enclosing him, forever, then shoving a huge dildo through the ass opening of the bull costume, holding it in with a tight rubber harness. His wrists were bound by chain to the wall.

Damn, he has an itch in his upper back. He moves his arm to scratch, and is jarred when he can't move his arm. He moves the other. Fuck it, it's not going anywhere. Opening his eyes, he sees...blackness? Shit!

zach is held down, his head is covered. He smells rubber. They've got him bound in chains with a hood on. Voices!
"Ah, he's awake," says his captor.

A deep voice answers, "Yeah, and he's hard again." A warm mouth covers his cock and begins slurping it down his throat. zach is pumped and he feels himself hardening more. Suddenly it stops.

"Well, my boy. Today we are going to make a mold out of you, for our future pleasure. When we're done, we might not need you any more, just your body."

"Sounds good to me," says the deep voice. "When do we begin?"

"Now. We'll take the fucker now."

Chains are loosened but the shackles remain. His hands are pulled forward, roughly. "Get up shithead," he's ordered. Fumbling around, zach tries to feel the edge of the bed and is swatted on his ass.

"Move it! Move it, come on, move it! Now!"

He gets up and trips, stumbling to the floor. "C'mon you fucking, clumsy shit. Watch your step!"

Watch his step? He can't see anything. No coffee, no breakfast, nothing. Oww! The chains pull between his toes. He shuffles his feet, pushing chains out of the way.

Geez, he must look like Marley's ghost, covered with chain and clanking with every step.

Roughly, the chain is grabbed and zach is led. He hears a door opening, and then goes down stairs, lots of stairs.

He is led slowly, feeling his way. He almost trips and is grabbed.

"Okay, buttfuck, turn around and on your knees." the voice echoes. "You're going to crawl down - backward."

This is a big space, he thinks. zach creeps his way step by step until he feels a concrete floor.

"Get your ass up." zach's chains are pulled and he is lifted by a powerful hand until he stands. "Now step back a couple of steps." He does. "Stop." He does.

A hand puts some grease all over his ass, up his hole, over his balls, twisting them in the process. He sucks air in between his teeth. "Now back up." He does as he feels something pressing against his asshole. "Push your asshole onto that dildo, fucker."

He does, he wants to do it slowly, but is pushed back onto a big dildo. His bunghole is dry, but the dildo is forced in, painfully. It seems to be on a hinged device. As it is straightened out, it forces him up on his toes. He finally hits bottom, on to an ass-shaped seat. zach's ass relaxes and the pain stops.

On his toes, his weight is supported on that seat. He couldn't get out of here if he wanted to, because he couldn't raise himself high enough with his feet to get off that damn dildo.

His cuffs are loosened and removed. His ankles are attached to the floor.

"You can't get out of here, so don't try nothing," the deep voice says. zach's hood remains in place.

Deep Voice announces, "Rubber Daddy Bear here is going to make a cast of you, naked, including your head and all.

"You'll be encased in three inches of plaster, and then we might take you out, or we might not. We'll use your mold to make two statues of you, a soft rubber statue, and a hard concrete statue.

"We'll take that concrete statue and dip it in black rubber and in flesh rubber to make two one piece solid rubber suits which will have every ripple and crease in your body, every pore of your skin. These skins will be you. If you're lucky, you may get to wear these suits.

"The rubber shrinks when it gets cooked, and the plaster shrinks a bit too, so these suits will be your second skin and fit you tighter than a glove, covering every inch of you. They will be glued onto your body, onto your face, and sealed to your cock and balls and to your asshole and you'll become rubber boy."

A creamy substance is being put on zach's body. Ouch, he is being shaved. His chest, under his arms, his back, arms, legs, and then someone grabs his balls. Carefully the lather is put on, partially wiped away, and the razor is deftly used to clean every wisp of hair. Cold water is poured over his body, shaking him with its suddenness. Towels rub his skin to remove excess water.

"Now, boy, feel your body, run your hands over your legs, over your cock." Other hands touch smoothly, caressing him. It soothes him, as more liquid splashes on his body.

It's not water, it stings. He winces and smells the alcohol. Are they sterilizing him?

"God damn it, what have I gotten into, let me go." A hard smack to his ass lets zach know where he stands. On his toes, supported by a giant dildo that he can't get off, stark naked, with two big men guarding him. What the hell can he do? Panic. He's just been shaved and they're going to encase him in plaster.

Another sharp blow with a paddle on his ass does nothing for zach's confidence. Dad didn't tell him what to do when he was so stupid as to get into something like this. "Why did I answer that ad?" he asks himself. "No one knows I'm here. This might just be it," he thinks.

OOOH, what's that? Something cold has been slapped across zach's chest. It's smoothed on. Another. These must be plaster strips like they use for casts, he figures. One after another. The strips are laid across his stomach, across the top of his shoulders. His legs are moved forward and the cuffs are removed.

The cold plaster strips are run across his legs, halfway to the back. One after another across the front until his legs are covered, even the tops of his feet. Strips are put between his toes. His front is almost finished, except for his arms and around his cock and balls. He wonders why they haven't been touched. He doesn't dare think about it.

They wait for a few minutes. The plaster warms up a bit as it sets. zach feels the tightening plaster next to his skin. At least he won't have to worry about hair being pulled out by the plaster. He has none now, and his body does feel great without hair. He relaxes a bit. Something creamy and sticky is put on the edge of the plaster. They track along the edge of the plaster with what smells like Vaseline.

After they finish with the Vaseline, they start laying the plaster strip by wet strip on zach's shoulders, down his back, under his arms, across his buttocks, around the shaped seat, down his legs. They're making a front and back shell, he concludes. And he will get out, he starts to realize. But when?

zach's body is rigid now and it feels so heavy, weighed down by the wet plaster. The dildo seat is rotated up and they plaster the back of his legs, the soles of his feet. He is now stiff and warm from the setting plaster.

"The fucker might need a drink," says Daddy. A straw is put between his lips and he gulps down the cold, refreshing water.

"I have to take a piss, Sir" zach says.

"Go to it, boy." He lets loose, and he hears it splashing onto the floor.

He is ordered to hold his left arm slightly out from his body, palm down. The plaster strips cover his arm to the wrist. He holds his right arm out and it is covered, too. He hears chains being attached to him.

God damn, they've embedded eye bolts or something in the plaster. zach's body is raised off the floor with a winch. Another chain is attached to an eye bolt over his kidney. He is pulled up, and the dildo pulls out painfully, making a loud vulgar ploop as his asshole slams shut.

The winch pulls his ass up so zach is almost horizontal now. What the hell difference does it make? He can't move anything except his fingers and his hooded head. Something is rubbed all over his exposed rear... There they go again, shaving. He feels the razor gliding over his ass cheeks. zach's cheeks are spread and the razor brushes his bung hole. His body shivers - or tries to. Once more the alcohol makes him wince. He can't do a damn thing about it. They can do whatever they want; and they will, he's sure. His ass cools as the alcohol evaporates. No, not another! zach thinks, as they lube his rear and insert a dildo.

"That'll make it easier to locate a butt plug," says Deep Voice. Someone rubs his head. Plaster strips are laid across zach's ass, and his cheeks are spread aside so strips can be put in his crack.
These rubber suits they talked about start to capture his imagination. Over his feet will be boot gloves separating each toe. The suit will hug his ass, right to his hole and even into him, covering not only his body outside but some of his body inside, too. It's a delicious thought.

He might like this after all. They aren't hurting him. He certainly is vulnerable now, but they are being careful.

Another tube is put into his mouth and zach sucks in warm chicken broth. It tastes pretty good right now. "Your fucking asshole is done." trumpets Deep

Voice.

"Don't he look cute with that double dildo stickin' outta that white plaster ass? Now for the hands." It's Daddy talking as some goop is slathered onto zach's hands. It's soft, warm and mushy. It's pushed between his fingers.

"That stuff is so good," says Deep Voice, "that it will even copy your fingerprints." After the goop solidifies, they put plaster strips over that. Now all that's left are zach's cock and balls and his head. His head! What are they going to do with his fucking head?!? He'll know soon enough as they talk about his head. zach feels the tugging of his hood, and it is ripped off his face.

zach can now see for the first time. He is in a cavernous basement with lights shining on him. He glances down at his immobile plaster-covered body. In the mirrors he sees the double dildo sticking out of his ass, partially covered with plaster. He wiggles his ass in his carapace and feels the tightness as the dildo moves a bit. The plaster has shrunk slightly and is pressing tightly, heavily, all over him. zach sees his tormentors sitting in the dark.

"Time for a break, boy. Just relax, smoke 'em if you got 'em." They both guffaw, relishing the sight before them. "You'll love the next step, boy, cuz that's when we cover your whole head, and you'll be buried deep in plaster. First, we cover your head with this dental goop, we stuff it up your nose and into your mouth, we cover your eyes with it and plug your ears with it."

They're going to kill me, zach thinks. But they wouldn't even have to do anything, with me sealed in this plaster. They wouldn't even have to bury me. I'd just be a bulbous modern sculpture hanging in their living room.

The men could see his fear. "Hey, boy, calm down. You'll be all right. You see, we put these breathing tubes in, and we'll even give you something to drink before we bury you," Deep Voice said, laughing rudely. Daddy and Deep Voice have rubber hoods on as they come over. Deep Voice is naked, huge and hairy. Daddy is a big guy but not towering like Deep Voice. "Time to begin. You gonna shave 'im?"

Daddy nods as he brings out a bowl, clippers and a razor. The clippers do their work and trim down his hair. Then they're run over his eyebrows, his 'stache. The hair falls over the plaster, and Deep Voice brushes it off. zach's head and face are lathered, and all his hair comes off. He loved his dark blond hair; he combed it and brushed it every day, but his eyebrows? How would he explain that at work? They wash him clean.

"Don't he just look squeaky and shiny!"

Again the alcohol, and then some grease to cover his eyelashes. Deep Voice is mixing a bowl of powder and water, swirling it around. He brings it over and they start putting this pink goo on the top of zach's head, around his neck, on his forehead. It slides a bit until it gels. They put it on his cheeks. It's warm and starts to set, but he can still move. It's like rubber: soft, plastic, comfortable.

Deep Voice kisses zach, and Daddy comes over and gives him a deep, loving kiss, too, whispering, "Love you, boy." Then he slaps a handful of glop over zach's ears, poking it into the ear canal.

Daddy winks and smiles through his black rubber hood and slaps a glob over zach's eyes. Two tubes are put up his nose, and he is ordered to test them as Daddy clamps his hand over zach's mouth. What a relief-he can breathe through the tubes. He is given a straw, and he sucks the water greedily. This will be his last for a while.

Another glob goes over his nose, and someone pushes the stuff into his nostrils. He breathes through his nose. Someone smacks a big, deep kiss on him. "OPEN YOUR MOUTH,' is the last muffled order zach hears. Again, a mouth comes over his, but this time the mouth transfers goo into his. It fills his mouth. It covers his tongue and is pushed between his gums and his teeth, it covers his lips.

Another kiss into the wet goo. It sets quickly. zach dares not swallow. He is being cast with this rubbery goo filling every opening. He feels more stuff being put on his face. It is dark, it is quiet, it is still. He can't move, he can't do anything except dream. He feels movement as they encase his rubbery head in layers of plaster.

Daddy and Deep Voice look at the lumpy white apparition before them - all white, except for two black rubber tubes hanging from his huge head, all white except for the fleshy cock now stiffening at his crotch that is the final target. They are pleased with their handiwork and they know that while zach may be worried about his future, his cock loves what's going on.

A rubber ball stretcher is put around his scrotum, making his balls tight and thrusting straight down from his body. zach realizes his manhood is to be covered, too. A warm mouth begins sucking on his cock. Sucking him fervently. zach has never felt like this before. He is warm and cocooned, protected. He may even be enjoying it. He feels his cock get rock hard, and then some goo goes on his balls. Both cock and balls are sticking straight out.

His final opening is to be sealed after a catheter is inserted. zach feels the catheter sliding down his cock, and shivers when it passes through the sphincter. Then someone fondles him. His cock and balls are stretched, covered with goo and finally embedded in plaster.

zach hangs from the cellar ceiling with chains reaching to the heavy steel eye bolts embedded in his form, an immense lumpy white plaster anthropomorphic shape. He smells something through his nostril tubes and falls to sleep...

He shook the sleep from his eyes. Where was he? By the side of the road? His bike was parked beside him. It couldn't have been a dream, he thought, that total encasement in plaster. His cock and balls and face being coated with cold goo. Even his mouth being filled, every crevice, even around his tongue. He almost gagged at that thought. Yet, here he was alone, somewhere on this stunningly beautiful day. He rubbed his head. He had no hair. He felt his eyebrows, they were gone. He pulled up the sleeve of his jacket, shorn of every tuft of hair.

He got up and looked in the mirror of his bike. God damn, he was bald and shiny. How would he explain that at work? Fuck all! Who the hell did they think they were, taking off all his hair!?! He had to take a piss. As he pulled out his dick, he swore again, all his crotch hair was gone. His cock hardened as he stood there feeling himself with heightened sensitivity. He touched his arm and felt the smoothness of his bare skin devoid of any rough spots. He opened his jacket and rubbed his chest. Nipples stood up, sensitively waiting for him to tweak them. zach was getting horny. He lay on the ground beside the tree away from the road, unbuttoned his tight leather pants and played with himself. Feeling his new hairlessness, stimulating his thoughts, remembering the time he had. Remembering the excitement of being covered in rubber, of the closeness of the plaster encasement, of the dildo up his ass, of the feeling of having his cock slathered in clammy goo, of his mouth being filled. He came as he saw himself in his tight, skin-colored rubber suit. WOW! That was terrific.

Now what? He was wondering if his cap and leather mask were around. Opening his saddlebags, he saw a note.

"Suckhead," it began. "You got a taste of being my rubber boy. Leave the life you now have. Cut off everything and join me forever, or fuck off. Make your choice on Saturday. Call me at exactly 1:00 pm or forget it."

Cheez. That was it. One life or the other, no compromise.

It was seven AM. Still time to go home. He drove around till he came to a 7-11, got some gas, coffee, a crusty doughnut, and asked directions. The guy looked strangely at him standing there, no eyebrows and all, but he responded and zach took off on his bike. Getting to his big, elegant apartment, he looked around and sat down for a minute before deciding what to do. He was doing OK. Great salary, good job, great benefits. He had a decent relationship with his brothers and some of the guys. He had a great body, good looks, although altered now. He loved his life, his apartment, his gear, his neighbors. Dammit, he liked where he was.

zach showered, put on a starched shirt, that great new tie, and his pinstripe suit. He concocted a story about being surprised by his friends in an initiation rite and was shorn of his hair. He looked odd, bald like that. Would Sam, his boss, believe him? What about the big sales meeting with the company's biggest client? He was the point man.

Thoughts rushed through his mind. As he walked to his BMW, his shorts brushed against his naked balls, and he started to harden - other thoughts flooded his mind. Goose bumps raised on his body, chills up his spine. Give all this up, for what? Rubber? It was fun while it lasted, but a new, insecure life built around rubber...Shit no!

The call went in precisely at 1:00. The instructions were clear. "Be at my door," he said, "tomorrow at 9:00 AM. Bring your leather gear and your bike, nothing else." Click.

zach obeyed. Like the last time, he stood at the door and rang the buzzer. He lowered his head as the door opened and the voice said, "You are mine to do what I want and what I say. Once you come in, you will not leave without my authorization. If you ever disobey, you will be discarded. You will seal this agreement in blood." The voice paused. zach stood, silent.

"Enter."

zach kept his eyes lowered as he was guided to a chair before a small table. He was handed a scalpel, a pen, and a sheet of paper which read "Agreement of Indenture." He read the demanding agreement, wincing at some of the restrictions. He poked his finger with the scalpel and forced some drops onto a small crystal cup. Dipping the fountain pen into the blood he signed and dated the agreement. So did his new Master.

"See that hood? Put it on."

zach obeyed and pulled the rubber hood over his head. Made of soft latex, it had pinholes for eyes, nose holes, and a large open mouth. The lacings were pulled tight, and then Master said, "Now wear this," handing him a rubber suit.

zach pulled on the suit, stretching it to cover his body. It snapped as he pulled it over his thighs. It snapped as he lifted it over his bubble ass forcing the attached dildo into him. He pushed the dildo in until it was firmly seated in his asshole. It stretched tightly as he stuffed his arms into the sleeves and attached mitts. It squeaked as he lifted his rubber suit over his huge chest. He adjusted it and stood while his Master zipped it slowly, stuffing the rubber hood under the collar of the suit. Then a collar was tightened around his neck.

"Take my boots off and kiss my feet."

zach, still not looking at the face of his Master, went on his knees.

"Clean it, asswipe."

He licked the black boot, making it shine along the ankle. His tongue slid along the top of the sole and the heel. His lips surrounded each heavy lug of the boot, and he licked the mud from between the lugs. His nose touched and smelled the rubber as he washed the bottom of the boot with his tongue. His hood was getting dirty with mud and he tasted the gritty muck, swallowing each morsel.

"Now take it off, shithead."

He pulled off one heavy, black, hip-high rubber boot, shiny with his spit, exposing his Master's heavily tattooed leg and foot. He cupped the foot in his hand suddenly realizing that it was flesh colored rubber. Heavily tattooed, flesh-colored rubber. He pulled the foot up to his face, kissing it, he took each toe, covered individually in rubber, into his mouth and sucked on one after the other. He licked his Master's foot, savoring the rubbery feeling and smell. He was fascinated by the snake skin tattoos covering his Master's foot. His Master groaned as he licked the bottom of his foot. Every inch was tattooed. Was the rest of this powerful man covered with tattoos? Whap! He jumped as his ass was slapped with a rubber whip. He was getting harder by the stroke.

"Now do the same for the other foot, asshole."

He did. And he savored it.

"Now turd, suck my cock."

zach moved up and saw the massive thighs covered with snake skin tattooed rubber. His Master's cock stood straight out stretching its tattooed rubber sheath which he gleefully took into his mouth. He stroked this cock, tattooed with a serpent's head, gently, slurping it into his throat. He ran his tongue up and down the rubber-covered shaft and could feel it getting even harder. He ran his tongue down to the balls encased in separate tattooed rubber ball sacs. He suckled on these balls, rolled them around in his mouth as his Master began humping. He moved back to his big cock, swallowing it, running it down his throat. That beautiful rubber cock that he had given up his plush life for. zach loved the slick rubber shaft gliding down his throat. His Master grabbed his head and began fucking his face, sliding the shaft faster and faster down his throat.

His Master went stiff, his juices filled the tight rubber sheath, and zach could feel the warm man-juice in his throat. Shuddering, his Master came, as his cum slid around its sheath oozing into his rubber ball sacs and into his crotch.

zach continued to hold the softening shaft in his mouth. His Master pushed his head away.

"Stand, boy, and look at me!"

zach raised his eyes, and through the pinholes of his mask was allowed to look at this man, his man, for the first time. His eyes moved from the ample cock and balls to the man's stomach, where two snakes crossed their bodies, then to his big chest where their heads glared at one another. Up his rubber-covered neck, and then to his head, totally covered in a beautiful rubber tattoo over a mask shaped like a snake head. Here, standing before him, was his Master completely covered in a snake suit made of tight rubber. zach could see his Master nearly naked, but could not know what he looked like.

"Come to me, boy."

He took zach into his arms, and he kissed zach through their rubber masks, swirling tongues, sucking each other. "Well, my boy, you will get into more rubber than you ever imagined. Tonight, you will be the centerpiece of our club party..."

One of the slaves ordered to contribute to the party's preparation kept this account...

Master's parties were famous, and rubber lovers came from all over the world. Each party had more surprises than the last. zach was not the only slave, but he was the newest and was to have the special place of honor. william, tom, sam, and zach were now being prepared. Each had been shaved top to crotch.

william was to be in the limelight later after all the rubbermen showed up, so he was put away for the moment. He positioned himself over a short rubber stool on wheels with an enormous black dildo sticking out of it. Master's aide the Master Dresser, barked at him, "you're taking too long, muther fucker!" and he pushed down on william's shoulders, forcing the dildo painfully, completely, into his ass. william cried out and he was slapped across the face, hard. Now on the dildo stool, william began rising as the Master Dresser pumped at the hydraulic lift. His toes barely touching the floor, william was stuck there. Handed a thick black rubber hood with nose tubes only, william was ordered to pull it on. Master Dresser grabbed a thick rubber collar off the wall and tightened it around william's neck. Rigid and high, the rubber collar sealed him in his rubber hood and kept his head from moving. The chair was wheeled into a cage where william's arms were cuffed to the ceiling bars. He would be bound in his steel cage on the big black rubber dildo until the party was ready for him.

tom was next. Master Dresser coated his body with a layer of water-based lube until every muscle of his powerful body glistened. He had to be well-lubed for what was coming. Master Dresser tossed over a heavy one-piece full rubber suit molded to tom's body. The two of us were ordered to stretch open the mouth hole since that was the only way in, while tom stuck his feet through and wriggled into the suit. We stretched it over his feet, pulled it over his round, smooth butt, tugged and smoothed it over his hard washboard belly, and stretched it to tearing as we forced his big shoulders into the suit. Then we lifted the hood over his face, the mouth of the suit swallowing him whole like a shiny black serpent. The mouth snapped shut over his face.

Master Dresser took a mouthpiece molded to tom's mouth and forced it between his lips. tom moved it around his mouth until the lips, teeth and tongue fitted perfectly. The plug overlapped tom's lips. Carefully, Master Dresser wiped any lube from the mouth of the hood and dabbed rubber cement over the outer edge of the mouth plug and the inner edges of the mouth opening. He held the edges apart as they dried, then carefully laid the lips of the hood over the lips of the mouth plug and sealed them smoothly together.

Dipping a small brush in spirit gum, Master Dresser lifted open the small eye holes and dabbed the gum along the orbit of tom's eyes. He carefully glued the mask around tom's eyes and into his nostrils, sealing the mask to tom's face so it could not slip. Now tom was totally sealed into his one piece suit. tom's cock and balls were proudly sticking out of the attached sheath. Master Dresser pulled tom's ballsac down and glued on a thick four inch black rubber ball stretcher making tom's balls stick straight down from his body while his eight-incher stuck straight out from his shiny rubber crotch. A black rubber dildo was pushed into tom's ass forcing the suit's attached black rubber sac in, too.

tom was sealed in shiny, thick, black rubber, his rubber encasement covering his body inside and out. His voice now became a gurgle, as slight noises burbled through the fitted black rubber gag sealed to his mask. He started to sweat, and his lubed suit slipped slightly on his body, giving him an electric charge which made his cock stand out straighter. Now Master Dresser took a sterile metal tube with a rounded bulge from the autoclave and inserted the stainless steel catheter into tom's stretched dick. tom stiffened as the cold steel entered his piss slit, as it pushed up his cock tube, and he jerked as the enlarged bulb forced itself through his sphincter. A little fluid dribbled out.

A smooth black leather hood was pulled over the rubber hood now sealed on tom's face. Holes for his nose, mouth and eyes in the leather hood overlaid exactly the holes in his heavy custom-fitted rubber mask. The leather hood was zipped and lacing was pulled tightly, compressing his face in a soft black leather vice. "You okay, asshole? You're going to have this on a long time tonight, and we don't want it hurting you, do we?" tom nodded OK.

There was clanking as an assistant wheeled over what looked like a suit of armor. This was to be tom's prison for the night. Seeing this, tom's eyes sparkled through the rubber and leather masks. Was that fear, or excitement? We couldn't tell as his eyes danced in his tiny eye slits. We were ordered to polish tom. We rubbed flowing white liquid all over tom's tight rubber-covered body, highlighting his wonderfully thick rubber-encased muscles. The blue lights overhead made the rubber shine in all the right places, especially the glint of the stainless steel tube now sticking out of his stiff dick. tom, ordered to stand on this wheeled stainless steel dolly, was too slow and he jumped as a studded rubber paddle smashed his ass with a resounding crack. Tears welled up in his hooded eyes and a guttural whimper issued from his plugged mouth.

"Shut the fuck up, jellyfish! Or we'll take you out of tonight's events and throw you outta here."

Stiff steel gloves were attached to tom's hands and the arm pieces were screwed to the gloves and bolted to rotating rings at the arm holes. It seemed a little peculiar that the gloves were positioned the way they were. A stiff steel collar was taken out and positioned around tom's neck, forcing his head high as it was set in the neck ring. tom's dick and ass, his head, and his rubber-covered tits were the only things left exposed.

A crotch piece was fitted to tom's crotch with holes through which his rubber-sheathed dick and his stretched ball sac protruded. There was also a nice round hole for the ass. But that was soon sealed up as Master Dresser took out the rubber butt plug and inserted a thick, 12-inch-long, shining steel dildo into tom's ass, slipping it into the rubber sleeve in his rubber undersuit. tom groaned as six large bolts were used to seal the dildo onto the metal suit.

A beautifully-crafted stainless steel cock-and-ball sheath was carefully fitted over the rubber sheath and rings were tightened around the balls and the cock sealing them into their rubber and steel prisons. The catheter stuck out from the suit and the metal sheath was bolted with six hex bolts to the crotch piece of the steel suit. A setting ring was fitted over the catheter which firmly anchored the catheter onto the sheath. tom's eyes flitted as he strained to see himself in the mirrors around the room. He was now a sweating rubbered metal man in his suit, brilliantly shining except for his black head, but that soon changed.

Master Dresser fitted an open-faced helmet onto the collar and settled it in its channel to let tom turn his head stiffly. It was strange seeing that handsome black rubber face peering out of that metal helmet. Now the final pieces. A face piece was set on tom's face and bolted on forcing two metal tubes into tom's nostrils. A mouth piece was placed over tom's mouth and a steel tube was attached to the catheter and fitted into the mouth piece being set into place with two bolts. Three tubes protruded from tom's steel mouth. One was the catheter, forcing tom to drink his own piss. Two other tubes were for liquids and breathing. tom could still see out of the tiny eye slits in the face piece.

Finally, a silver serving tray was brought out and tom's hands were positioned and bolted to hold the tray. tom was to be the drink server, a living tray moving about on a wheeled dolly. Master Dresser pulled out a controller which was used to drive the dolly, and tom, now finished and being polished by assistants, was slowly wheeled to the door and turned, ready for his service for the night.

zach could only imagine what tom felt like, unable to move a muscle, to change positions, to be bound intensely by his steel and rubber, sweating like a pig with that big hard silver dildo forced up his ass. zach wondered what was in store for him.

But it was sam's turn. sam's preparations were simple. He was put into a one piece silver-colored rubber suit. His hood was a silver pig face with no eye holes, except he had a huge red rubber ball forced into his mouth before the hood was attached. His hands and feet were pig's hooves in black rubber. The suit had a cock-and-ball sheath on the front and a big black rubber dildo attached inside. Master Dresser's assistants pulled the suit onto sam, forcing the plug into him. They put the red ball gag into his mouth and pulled the pig's head on, set it inside the collar of the silver rubber suit and finished zipping up the suit. The hand and foot hooves were attached and glued onto the suit. Finally, sam was trussed up with rubber straps and tied onto a table to wait while zach was prepared.

zach was ordered to the center of the room where he saw an eight-foot-high by five-feet-wide rubber mat on the floor. It wasn't just a piece of rubber material, but a half-inch thick slab of black rubber, the center shaped to his body. A dildo protruded from the indentations. "Sit on that, shithead."

He sat on the huge rubber dildo forcing it into himself, past his sphincter, deep into his body. He groaned as it entered, overcoming his body's resistance. he finally got it all the way in, and the shape of the mat fitted along his ass crack. he lay down into the form, and it covered the bottom half of his body perfectly fitted to every fold and indentation. his muscled back felt comfortable as each muscle found its place. his ass cheeks fit, as did his thick thighs. Then they started pouring black stuff onto the large square mat and all over him. he knew by the light ammonia smell that it was black liquid latex and that he would be sealed into his rubber bed and become as one with the rubber. It coated him and the whole surface of the mat, filling any spaces in the molded shape. it was cool as it started to set up. Over his head they had brought another large black rubber mat to place over him. Embedded in it was his body form. He was going to become a zach sandwich!

"This, my boy, will fit you perfectly, since it was made on your plaster form. The arms are straight out, so stick your hands into the holes as far as you can."

The huge shaped rubber mat was being lowered and touched his chest first. he found the arm holes. Squeezing his arms, dripping with black liquid latex, into the fitted holes wasn't all that easy from that position, but his hands finally slipped into the gloves built into the rubber mat. The mat was lowered more and someone was playing with his cock and balls dripping in black liquid rubber, inserting them into the built-in sheath. His toes and feet were put into position, and the mat continued to be rolled on top of him, now covering his neck. Someone dabbed liquid black rubber over his face to seal it to the rubber sheet enfolding and encasing his head. He wriggled his face and felt his lips entering the lips and nose of the rubber mask on top of him until it was a perfect fit. He opened his eyes and was weighed down with hundreds of pounds of thick rubber sheeting that was totally covering him. He was now the zach Rubber Sandwich with his face and arms protruding from the rubber sheeting like a bas relief in black.

He was to be one with the rubber, vulcanized to it. The thick top rubber sheet was being sealed to the thick bottom rubber piece. The only way zach was going to get out of this thing was to be cut out of it or be sealed in forever, he thought. Master Dresser and his assistants were on top of the mat squeezing out all the air, sealing it completely. Someone was playing with zach's dick as he felt the special feeling of a catheter being forced into him. He imagined himself in this rigid black rubber mat with arms, toes, face and dick sticking out. What were they going to do with him? He was starting to get hot in his rigid prison. He heard people working around him when suddenly he was lifted into the air totally supported by this rubber frame.

Guests were starting to arrive and were kept in the foyer while final preparations were being made in the great hall. They milled around, getting drinks from the bar. Most were in black rubber, but there were some in red, green or blue. The uniform crowd was represented by men in full rubber military uniforms and sailor suits. Some had capes, most had masks or hoods on, here and there were guys with gas masks and tubes and long black rubber coats. The rubber smell was heady, and they were getting excited.

The great doors were opened, and the wildly-dressed guests were greeted by the stainless steel waiter serving hors d'oeuvres from a large sterling silver tray. On the table filled with food was a silver rubber piggy with a big red apple in its mouth surrounded by fruits, vegetables and other delectables. The pig's hard dick was available for anyone wanting a sucker, too.

On the wall twelve feet up was a huge black rubber hanging of a muscular man captured in rubber. There were several tubes hanging from his big rubber dick. One was marked lite beer, one was marked dark beer, and the third was marked recycled. The tubes went to taps just above the bar and any guest could tap in for a fresh beer or recycled beer. The kegs rested on chains over the sculpture, and the tubes went into the sculpture with two valves over the tits and a third valve in the belly button. The three tubes then came out of the cock and hung eight feet down to the bar.

Master was dressed in his complete rubber tattoo suit, cod piece shorts and a great rubber cape draping on to the floor. The cape was black on the outside and brilliant royal purple inside which shone in the spotlight. Master stood at his throne at the raised dais beside the stage and boomed a welcome to the crowd, which let out a roar in greeting. "Let the Party begin!" he bellowed.

The room had been fitted out as a dungeon with devices and racks for play - the metal cages were there for anyone to use, as were the ropes and pulleys hanging from the ceiling, the tables, benches, and the rubber covered mats on the floor, and the beds. This was a wide open party.

"To get you moving, we're going to have some entertainment!" Master's voice resounded.

The stage lights moved to the side of the stage, and a figure in a cage was wheeled out to the center. Master Dresser opened the cage, unshackled muscle boy william inside, and took off the tight collar and hood that kept him in the dark until now. The dildo stool was lowered and william was ordered to lift himself off the black dildo. When it plopped out noisily, the rubbered crowd roared with laughter. The slave was given a small eye cover with a rubber band to cover his eyes. a long tube was forced into his mouth and tied with a rubber band on the back of his shaved head. He was led a few steps to a platform and made to stand on it. His hands were shackled on the chains overhead for support and he was lifted up over eight feet above the stage. A large vat was wheeled onto the center of the stage, and the slave was positioned above it.

"Now you will see the experience you all wish for! This slave will be totally immersed in this vat of thick black rubber."

Slowly, william was lowered into the vat. The warm black goo surrounded his toes and ankles. He sank into it up to his knees and he started to panic. Master soothingly reassured him as it reached his crotch and covered his cock and balls and oozed into his ass crack. It filled his belly button, and covered his chest. he stiffened and raised his head as it covered his neck and started over his chin. He grasped the breathing tube harder with his teeth as the thick black rubber sloshed over his mouth and pushed up his nostrils. He shivered as it rose over his eyes and bubbled over his head.

He was now completely embedded in warm thick black liquid rubber. Slowly the crane lifted the dripping, shining rubber man. The excess liquid rubber drained off his black shimmering body.

Heat lamps shone on his body and fans blew warm air over him. He began drying and the rubber began shrinking, tightening on every inch of his body. His dick became engorged and rock hard, and the rubber grew with him. Now he felt people over him. He had been lowered to the stage, and assistants were attaching dildos all over his body. On his forehead, on his mouth, on the back of his head. His belly, knees and arms sported dildos. Black rubber dildos of all sizes all over him. Someone stuck a big black double headed dildo up his ass, and it projected out of his body like his own cock. He was becoming the dildo man. Once again he was lifted and positioned over the vat of black liquid rubber.

Again he slowly descended into the black bubbling pool, sealing and permanently attaching all the dildos to his mighty body. Once again the crowd cheered as the dildo man emerged, dripping liquid rubber, and was dried. The rubber over his equips were removed, the shackles released, and he stepped off the platform to service the Master's rubber guests. As he walked down the stairs, the double dildo deeply embedded in him and sticking out jauntily wiggled from side to side stimulating him for a night of unimaginable passion. He could feel the dildo as he went down the stairs and relished the thought of being ass-to-ass with another guy sharing the same dildo, forcing it deeper into one another, each having the same experience. He knew the rubber guys would fuck themselves on his dildos. He imagined a RUBBERMAN settling his round rubbered ass on brian's mouth as the attached dildo forced the rose pucker open, slipping into his waiting ass until his ass was on the lips of dildoman while others attached themselves to the dildos on his hands and belly. He could see that bubble ass approaching his face, wriggling and humping his face with ecstasy. He was in for a great night. All over his body the black rubber became a little tighter as it hardened and cured. tom the shiny, black, rubber, dildoman.

Now the lights focused on the wall hanging, to zach, who was to be the finale, the centerpiece of the party. The blue spots highlighted the wall sculpture now moving into the center of the room. Black rubber tubes hung from his dick and swung as the remarkable rubber tapestry was moved. Heavy chains through huge grommets supported the heavy piece as it was lowered in the center of the room. When it reached eye level, it suddenly moved. The hands moved, the face twisted, the crowd suddenly realized that there was someone embedded deep in that sculpture: they didn't know that zach was totally sealed in, attached to the rubber mats.

Master's voice boomed again, "I present the zach Sandwich for your pleasure. Enjoy him, have fun."

The rubber crowd could now see three tubes hanging from his ass as well as three tubes coming from his dick. zach was lowered into their midst and they started to play with him kissing him through his heavy rubber lips of the mask sealed to his face, turning the spigots on his tits and belly, twisting the tits of the man inside, twisting zach's sensitive tits to get their fill. To drink the beer, virgin or recycled, they had to suck it out of the short tubes coming out of zach's dick. Warm mouths sucking his dick and groping hands twisting his spigots. His dick stiffened.

his outstretched rubber arms grabbed and held onto the man deep-throating him. zach could barely make out his rubber covered face in the darkening room. Someone was forcing an enema into him with an online bulb from a reservoir of soapy water. Another was pumping up the black rubber blowup dildo in him. He groaned with the water entering his bowels and his shit tube being forced wider. he couldn't believe the feelings - someone sucking his tubed cock and and another playing with his low-hanging balls. he was bouncing on his chains being loved and attacked by lusty rubbered men thrashing in sexual frenzy all over him. Suddenly, the third tube up his ass was released and the enema gushed out of him as his bladder was being sucked dry. Relief, for now.

Rubbermen stripped the steel waiter of some of his armor, pulling out the long steel dildo and shoving their dicks through the steel armor and into his rubbered body. Sweaty rubber guys fucked themselves on the face, head, arms and legs of dildoman, poured whipped cream, strawberries, nuts, and chocolate sauce on the silver pig and lapped it up. Thirsty rubbermen sucked on zach's cock to drink the fluids coming through the rubber sculpture, twisting the tit taps on and off, turning the enema hose on again and again and then draining him. Everywhere, sweaty black rubber bodies groping, kissing, pissing, giving, receiving enemas, fucking each other.

zach, the thick black rubber sandwich, was in heaven, enjoying the most incredible night he'd ever had or could ever imagine.

About the Author

Tim Brough can't leave well enough alone. He keeps turning out books even though he ought to know better. After all, he and Papa Joel exist only to serve me. But no - he goes gallivanting all over the country from here in Philadelphia leaving no more than an extra bowl of food and water to keep me company while signing books for his readers. So far, those titles include the kinky story collections *Black Gloves White Magic* and *Sgt. Vlengles' Revenge.* He chased red hankies at events until he could complete *First Hand: An Erotic Guide To Fisting* when he should have been playing chase the toy mouse with me!

And to what end? So you kinky types get valuable information and your rocks off? He should be playing with me, scratching my back and filling my water-dish. I demand that you fetish humans leave my staff alone!

Submitted by House Diva, Sophie Cat
Dec 19, 2006.

www.TimBrough.com
fetish books for bent readers

A Boner Book

Index

Symbols

A

B

C

S

T

V

W

Z

www.ingramcontent.com/pod-product-compliance
Lightning Source LLC
Chambersburg PA
CBHW051837020726
47502CB00005B/1832